The Terrible Thing is ultimately what put me here.
And The Parents were mostly responsible
for The Terrible Thing.

When Easter Deetz goes looking for her sister, Julia, she ends up pinned under a giant boulder with her legs crushed into tomato paste. Bored, disappointed, and thoroughly dismembered, Easter slowly bleeds to death in The Woods with only sinister squirrels to keep her company.

While The Something Coming draws closer, memories of Easter's family surface like hallucinations: a mumbling father who lives alone in the basement; a terrifying grandmother who sits in her enclosed porch all day; an overly loving mother who plays dead in the bathtub on Sunday nights.

As the story of her life unspools, Easter realizes she's being stalked, making it very difficult for her to bleed to death in peace. Will The Something Coming save her? Or do her in entirely?

the Lonely

AINSLIE HOGARTH

flux
Woodbury, Minnesota

First Edition
First Printing, 2014

Book design by Bob Gaul
Cover design by Kevin R. Brown
Cover images: iStockphoto.com/8300542/©2windspa
iStockphoto.com/19721817/©franckreporter

Flux, an imprint of Llewellyn Worldwide Ltd.

Library of Congress Cataloging-in-Publication Data
Hogarth, Ainslie.
  The lonely/Ainslie Hogarth.—First edition.
      pages cm
  Summary: "After she discovers The Terrible Thing, Easter Deetz goes looking for her older sister, Julia, but ends up pinned under a boulder in the woods, reliving memories of her family as The Something Coming draws closer"—Provided by publisher.
  ISBN 978-0-7387-4133-8
[1. Death—Fiction. 2. Sisters—Fiction. 3. Mental illness—Fiction. 4. Family problems—Fiction.] I. Title.
  PZ7.H68319Lon 2014
  [Fic]—dc23
                                            2014014106

Flux
Llewellyn Worldwide Ltd.
2143 Wooddale Drive
Woodbury, MN 55125-2989
www.fluxnow.com

For my Grandma and my Auntie Phyllis,
who are both wonderful people and
not fucking bitches at all.

The End

Just to warn you, I die at the end of all of this. So don't get too attached to me or anything. I bleed to death, and it's gruesome. So if you're squeamish or don't like to see bad stuff happen to kids, then you should probably just stop now. Because what happens is that I bleed slowly all day long. I get pale and desperate and cry and throw up. And I'm just a kid so I don't deserve any of it. I'm "too young to die." Even though I'm just as susceptible to being crushed by a giant rock as anyone.

Some people, though, they can't handle that kind of thing. Because kids are pure and innocent, full of rarest unicorn blood, and their guts are like pearls or diamonds or some other naturally occurring treasure sliced from Mother Nature.

The bleeding is kind of fun though. As it drains from your brain and out through the place where your legs used to be, you start to feel like you're floating on a million silvery needles, prickling. Like nothing matters anymore because it doesn't because you're stuck under a rock and you're going to die. Which is more of a relief than you're comfortable admitting. So you don't admit it. Instead you carry on to no one about how much you want to live, despite your crushed legs.

Of course you have your low/honest points. Points where you try to hide yourself with leaves, dig yourself deeper into the forest floor with the rotation of your shoulders, smear blood all over your face so you look worse off than you really are, try to convince the cigarette-smoking squirrels to do you in entirely before anyone has the chance to come and find you. But eventually you relax because you know you've got to. Know you've got to let the rock do its work, whatever that work may be. It'll kill you soon enough. Or not. Just a matter of time, says one of the squirrels as it strokes a rope of matted hair off your face, leaving a clean line on your forehead where it's dragged a tiny fingernail.

But maybe none of that really happened. Because you know that there's something not quite right with the way you see things anyway. Even before you started losing all the blood.

Before I moved into the June Room, me and The Mother and The Father and Julia lived in The House together for a very long time and if there's one family on the planet that's truly not worth knowing about, it's us. We're a Real, Live, Genuine Waste of Time. In fact, you could put that in lights above our front door. Soda pop and cotton candy and every face you've never noticed.

So let's see, if you don't like wasting your time and you don't like bad things happening to innocent, unicorn-blooded kids then you should really stop now, I mean it.

Though there is one thing. One juicy piece of family lore worth knowing about. My mom's niece is the kid who threw her fetus in a garbage pail at her high school prom. Her name is Denise and she has no memory of doing it. She doesn't even remember the prom. But some very hungry thing inside her obviously hasn't forgotten. She weighs 700 pounds and counting. She eats and eats and eats, all the time. Last year she officially ate herself immobile and now she's working on eating herself out of her own skin.

So we've got Denise in our family, and I guess she's worth knowing about. That's slightly before my time though. Denise had already embarked on the slowest suicide attempt in history before I was even born. And maybe that was the last interesting thing that would ever happen on The Mother's side of the family. That means The Father's side might be due for something soon.

The Beginning of the Story

I woke up this morning in dawn's fuzzy in-between. So the June Room was too quiet and paused and gray. Waking up into that still hour felt significant. As though something had fought the sleep drugs Mrs. Bellows insisted I swallow last night, and urged me to get out of bed, get dressed, and escape from her apartment building. So I did.

The lobby cat watched me tiptoe through one open eye, his fat face resting squished between scooped paws. He watched but didn't move, didn't do anything to blow my cover. His compliance in my escape made me feel even more sure that something wanted me to leave this place today. He was usually such a dickhead.

I walked toward The House, where The Mother and Father still lived but I didn't. Because now I lived in the June Room in Mrs. Bellows' Apartment Building with four other girls who'd done things to make their parents think they were a danger;

who were deemed unfit to live at home. Four other girls who were having The Lonely or something like it extracted somehow, through hot dinners and crafting and fresh air and vitamins and the same sleep drugs I got last night.

My old key in the lock; the inside of The House bluish and deep-sleep quiet so my every step was a shotgun blast. I opened cupboards and pawed through junk drawers. I took a box of cookies from the pantry and munched and examined how little had changed since I'd left.

Then I crept upstairs, opened the door to my favorite room, and found The Terrible Thing.

The Terrible Thing that was probably my fault that I didn't want to talk about or think about ever again. I wanted to be gone, away from The Terrible Thing. I wanted to erase this morning completely, hit reverse and watch it unravel, re-do it: instead of waking up at dawn I sleep till ten or later, go downstairs for breakfast with the other girls, or actually maybe I don't do that considering what happened last night in the Craft Room. The reason Mrs. Bellows made me take the pills.

Okay, never mind, unravel that too. I eat breakfast in my room. Alone, quietly dragging my elbows along the table's sharp corners, then sitting with Mrs. Bellows while she talks about loving myself, finding peace in this world. Later I put on my Sunday Dinner clothes, wave goodbye to Mrs. Bellows and she lets me go, hop on the side-of-the-house-bike, and ride it to The Parents' house. I hear the monotonous hum of the early news when I walk through the door. I see The Mother in the kitchen making dinner but she doesn't know I'm here yet. She glances at the clock and mutters, "Where is that girl" and I tuck myself further behind the doorframe. She presses her knuckles into her eye sockets and then walks to the basement door, knocks quietly, and whispers through the crack that dinner's nearly ready. The Father would have to emerge from the basement, which he hates to do. And she would feel like a disgusting nuisance, keeping her chin down, smiling, a rehearsed face, still wondering where I might be.

She liked to watch the news while she cooked. Associate all of the murders and rapes with the sensation of her hands heeling into a wad of premature pizza dough, feeling safe and warm and protected over our electric hearth as she knuckled into the edges of the undeveloped crust against the pan. Red tomato sauce ladled on top, slices of meat arranged neatly.

The Mother does care about me in her own selfish, over the top way. She told me once that God brought me to her. "God brought you to me" she said. "He wrapped you up in peach skin, inside out so the fuzzy stuff was touching you and the slimy stuff was on the outside. He delivered you personally, Easter. That's how special you are." Before, I had been immersed in my doughy little room; soft, wet, warm. Arms in legs up. Then he evicted me to life. Snatched me up and stuck a long, ruddy finger in my mouth, scooping the things out that would keep me from breathing and not bothering to close me up when he left. I wonder if he brought his flat hands down onto my chest, forearms stiff, pounding, pounding, pounding life into me. I wonder if I resisted—limp in his arms, splayed out in the unpredictable pattern of a burst water balloon. I excel at withholding. Resisting. Denying satisfaction. I bet it felt good.

Anyway.

After I saw The Terrible Thing all I wanted was Julia.

So I went into The Woods and started looking.

By anyone else's standards, The Woods wasn't really a woods at all. More like a leftover nail or nut or hinge that was supposed to have fit somewhere but never really did; it was a scrap that might have been snipped off like a bit of extra paper hanging over the perforated line.

Shaved on one side by a long, lazy highway and thinned out along the other into the backyards of neighboring houses, it was always filled with launched baseballs, the odd tire, bits of fast food garbage tossed from roaring cars.

It disturbed the neighbors that no one could really do anything with The Woods: buy it, dig up the trees and put a fence around the bare property. The neighbor told me that it was "a waste of space for anyone who wasn't looking to do nasty things like have sex or hide a body." Then I asked her if any bodies had actually been discovered there and she waved her thin-fingered hand in my face and told me not to be morbid.

I'd developed some of my own theories: buried treasure or a tunnel to Eloi. Perhaps it contained a pocket of earth in which a rare species of daffodil or insect or rodent had made its home. An endangered type of very sensitive squirrel that could only tolerate the excruciatingly bland conditions of the not-too-anything midsection of North America.

I hoped no one ever bought these woods, or turned them into anything other than what they were. Because to me they were precious. One spot, one little moment, a slice in the universe just big enough for a girl my age to slip sound-lessly into. A scar, a sliver, a sore, an accident. A blip. An extra bit of world where a person could hide from every-thing, including parts of their own head. And the trees made everything quiet down there. Like padding or insulation, carved into the shape of woods.

The creek path ran straight through The Woods, seared into it like a brand, presumably from end to end though I'd only really explored a length of the middle. It swelled in nice places and the pulse of the water rubbed a miniature sprawl of cliffs into the earth, good places to sit and look out over the water. Some sections of the creek were bright, quiet, warm places, where sunlight bounced off shallow rocks, furried in places with nearly invisible moss like baby body hair slickened by just-born gooeyness or soapy water. Other parts of the creek were darker, cold, wrapped up by trees all through the leafy months, the rocks as thoroughly chilled as frozen dinner rolls.

As I walked along the creek, I removed a green lighter from my pocket with a holographic hula girl on it jerking from side to side like a malfunctioning robot. Knowing how to smoke without looking like a jerk was a skill I had yet to master. And I had to master it before I saw Lev again, otherwise he might not think I was wonderful anymore. Lev is a boy who's got film over his eyes, milky and swirling; he's a sheer-skinned cave dweller, a subterranean humanoid who told me I was wonderful. He's also a smoker.

I told him that I smoked too. So I had to practice. Otherwise those frosted eyes would locate some other wonderful thing to harass at work instead of me.

I lit one of my stolen cigarettes. Nothing to it.

The smoke seemed to pry into my posture, lengthening my spine, straightening my back, moving my head up the way an elderly aunt might, trapping your chin in a cold finger and thumb, pushing her knobbled fist into your lower back. Elderly aunts find poor posture as offensive and disgusting as I might find a smear of snot in an old man's beard.

I found myself momentarily entranced, either by the smoke or the gushing of the creek, lulling me from myself, from thoughts of The Terrible Thing. I made my way through a few thin branches to a smooth patch of shaded rock along the very edge of the water.

Across the creek, the sun seared branched patterns of light onto the forest floor, forcing its way through in the shape of solid beams all filled with the magic of reflected dust, throwing unprepared patches of land on display. One particular section had a pair of boots on it, which I quickly realized were attached to a body, standing kitty-corner from me across the creek. Julia. Twenty feet away. Staring at me.

The sun had her fully by the feet, the rest of her body brushed over with leopard spots: a distorted, shadowy reflection of the twittering leaves overhead. She wore a black-and-red flannel shirt that she'd buttoned almost all the way to the top and didn't bother tucking into her stiff blue jeans. Julia the older sister is seventeen, and she got The Mother's genes. The long face, the delicate features, the nose squared at the end and small like a dice. Her skin glows, her limbs move edgeless like cooked green beans, and her hair is long and thick and red and beautiful. Her lips are full and pink and whenever we were apart I dreamed about spreading them on toast and eating them.

Her eyes were narrow and angry and I knew why. She'd been stuck in The Woods since The Fire and I was the one who'd done it. Abandoned her, scared and alone. All so that everything could just be normal and uncomplicated for me.

I knew I probably should have come down to see her, at least explain myself a little better, and a few times I almost did. But I just couldn't bear to see the look on her face, to see what being stuck in The Woods had done to her, to risk her following me back out and making me weird all over again.

That is, until I found The Terrible Thing. Once I found The Terrible Thing it was all I could do to stop myself from running into these woods, my woods, praying that she'd let me find her. Hers was the only face I could see right now, the only voice I could bear to hear.

"Hi Julia," I said.

I held the cigarette behind my back. I wanted to spring across the creek and grab her and never let go.

"Easter. Well. What a surprise. Sorry the place is such a mess, didn't get a chance to spruce it up before you came. Get it? Spruce? Because I live in The Woods now. You've banished me to The Woods."

"Oh stop, Julia."

"You stop! You stick me in these woods, you don't tell me how long I'll be here, you leave me alone with the strange sounds and the freezing cold with only the squirrels to keep me company—" She cut herself off, swallowed a mouthful of calm, and continued. "I didn't want to explode on you like that right away. I was really planning on giving you the cold shoulder until you cried. That would have been so much better."

"You must be pretty mad. The cold shoulder is your specialty."

"I am pretty mad, Easter."

I rolled my eyes and rubbed a sneaker against the rock as lightly as I could. I thought I could feel every individual grain of dirt rolling around beneath my sole.

Julia squinted at me.

>"What's the matter?" she said.
>"Nothing," I replied.
>"Can you just tell me what's wrong? It's obviously something."

And she took a step toward me, crushing a big berry with her foot. It spattered into the creek. I don't know why I was being so annoying. I wanted very badly to tell her everything; sharing with her used to be the only thing that made me happy. But somehow I was scared to tell her. Like to say The Terrible Thing out loud would be to make it undeniable. So instead I shook my head "no" and sniffed loudly.

>"Well it looks like Mrs. Bellows has done wonders for you. You look great, really. Much better than when I was around."
>"Don't be mean," I muttered.
>"No really." She made a little box with her fingers, centered it on me, and said, "You're the picture of sanity."

I could see how I must have looked between her squared fingers, hunched shoulders and droop-faced. I wouldn't speak until she put them away. After another long moment she finally took her fingers down.

"When did you start smoking?"

"I'm not smoking."

"Easter, I can see the smoke behind you. If you're not smoking then you should be more concerned about your pants being on fire."

"I don't know what you're talking about."

"Is this because of Lev? Does the wonderful Lev smoke?"

And I turned quiet again, and tried to put my face into an expression of The Terrible Thing, so she could read it there without my having to breathe the words to life. But instead she looked confused and more annoyed.

"Easter, would you just tell me what's wrong? This is so irritating!"

"I don't want to talk about it."

"Well then why did you come down here? Why did you even bother! Get out of here Easter! Scram! You're nothing but an intruder. A germ. A piece of sand agitating my oyster. But you're not a pearl; you're a tumor or a wart or a cyst. Get out!"

And just then, the glowing red cigarette that had been burning down behind my back seared my thumb, causing me to react: jump back and look down at my freshly reddened appendage. As soon as I looked back up, Julia was gone. The creek gushed cold and lonely in front of me.

The Terrible Thing, The Terrible Thing, The Terrible Thing.

There it was. In the bathroom. In The Tooth House. Just waiting for me. The Father wouldn't find it. He might not notice for days because he never, *ever* used *our* bathroom. Our cluttered, too-warm torture chamber.

"Julia?"

I knew she wouldn't respond.

"Julia, it was terrible. A terrible, terrible thing."

But she was gone.

I maneuvered my way back onto the path, brushed a few burrs off my sweater, and let the branches close up behind me. After a few minutes walking I wouldn't even know where to find that sunny spot again.

Before I could move much further, another distraction caught my eye, the sun reflecting off a glimmering something lodged between two rocks, deeper into the highway side of The Woods. I left the path and moved closer and saw that the glimmering something was a piece of metal, attached to a strip of leather wedged between two giant boulders. As I pulled and I gouged and I scraped around the intriguing item, the rocks which had seemed as stuck still as tiles shifted suddenly with a growl. I jumped and let out a little yelp, then looked around hotly. Julia probably heard that.

I pulled on it again angrily, revenge on an inanimate object, and this time it slipped right out, causing me to lose my balance and fall backward. I was so furious with the little item that I needed a moment of silence to compose myself properly, after which I recognized what it was: a horse bridle. With an ornately embellished *E* embossed into the side.

Elizabeth's bridle.

What the hell was Elizabeth's bridle doing out here? Elizabeth's bridle was supposed to be buried somewhere deep in Phyllis's basement, wedged between a crocheted photo album and a ring of mink pelts, not stuck between two rocks, two rocks that'd probably been wedged together since some Lonely woman gave birth to a Lonely girl, and that Lonely girl gave birth to Phyllis and Phyllis had The Mother and The Mother had me.

Then there was a low rumble in what sounded like the stomach of The Woods, a growling from somewhere far away. A pair of squawking birds flew from the treetops, startled. I was startled too. I'd never heard anything like it before. Then another growl, louder, and in a split second a giant boulder was tumbling over the rocks, about to splatter me into tomato paste.

Then

After the boulder came crashing down on me I passed out and became just a bleeding ornament in The Woods. As still and broken as a stone cherub, pushed over and cracked open.

Then. I remembered a cascading white tablecloth, like whipping cream stopped in its tracks. I'm under a banquet table at a wedding that I barely remember but have seen pictures of myself at. Friends of The Parents who they never see anymore. Both of my dimpled fists submerged in frosty metal dishes of melted ice cream like I was at the manicurist, listening to my name screamed, starting off as a yell then dissolving into a sob. I wanted to cry out to them but Julia said, "Shhhhh." That was the first time she got me in really big trouble.

I think about that tablecloth. A paused videotape. It's odd the way that things tend to stop looking like themselves when you take their motion away.

And suddenly I became very aware of my bleeding. A dark red

pool, throbbing with awkwardly spreading growth over and under the leaves on the ground. Speckles of gore caught light all the way to the path.

It didn't really hurt, but I could feel it, the blood escaping my body, and there was nothing I could do to stop it. It slipped from me smooth. Effortlessly. Like coins from an undiscovered hole in a pocket.

I looked up and saw the shape of Julia's head looking down at me over the side of the rock wall. Her hair hung around her face in ringlets of uncoiled snake skin.

"Julia!" I barely rasped. The effort caused me to cough uncontrollably.
"Can you move that thing?" she asked.

I squirmed a bit and tried to push it, but it was no use. My legs were mush, the boulder was halfway into the ground, and every effort to move on my part was exhausting. Just lying there, not moving, was ecstasy by comparison.

With effort, I shook my head no.

"Good," she said. "Now I'm going to go to The House to see what this terrible thing is."
"Wait, wait!" I growled.
"What?"
"How did you get Elizabeth's bridle down here?"
"Don't ask stupid questions, Easter."

And with that she was off. I tried to call again but all that came out of my mouth was a whisper of rattled phlegm.

What an asshole. Knowing Julia, she probably wouldn't be coming back. She would leave me here to die because that's what I was going to do to her. She was very vengeful, that sister of mine. I suppose I couldn't blame her though. Dying on a forest floor is exactly what I deserved.

So I just lay there. Coming to terms with the fact that I'd be bleeding to death for the rest of the day. I wish I could say that I was upset or worried or even scared, but I wasn't. I was almost looking forward to relaxing for a good long while. I just didn't want to spend the last few hours of my life lying in the dirt beneath a huge rock, enduring a long, slow death as opposed to the quick one I'd always dreamed of for myself.

The Terrible Thing. The Terrible Thing is ultimately what put me here. And The Parents were mostly responsible for The Terrible Thing. I started thinking that my slow and uncomfortable end was really all their fault and how, in that way, parents are just as responsible for your death as they are for your birth. They set you on the tangent along which you inevitably die. I wonder if thinking about this tangent is what it means to have your life flash before your eyes. It probably is, though I bet most people's life-flash tangents are populated with happier things: memories of barbequed hot-dogs over checkerboard tablecloths or the smell of a loved one's shoulder. Not just spite for negligent parents.

I should come clean about one thing first though: I don't have a fat cousin named Denise who threw her fetus in a garbage can. I lied. Sorry.

Babydom

I was born fourteen years ago in a big hospital in Canada. This is because The Parents were visiting Niagara Falls while The Mother was dangerously pregnant with me. When her water broke they were on the Maid of the Mist and no one noticed. I quickly became an emergency and The Mother had to be rushed to a hospital right there in Niagara Falls. From day one I was an inconvenience. But apparently I was a very cute baby so that helped my case a bit. According to The Mother anyway, I was very cute. And even Phyllis my Evil Grandmother says so. Of course when The Mother says the words, "You really were such a cute baby," she is exploding with pride and falling in love with me all over again, recalling memory-warmed images of my gummy smile and button nose. When The Evil Grandmother says it, she seems to be mourning the loss of my good looks.

What I always find disturbing about this story is that Julia had to endure a five-hour car ride with The Evil Grandmother to come and pick us all up at the hospital in Niagara Falls. The Mother didn't want to fly with such fresh meat. Julia would often torment me with horror stories about this car ride, tales of her having to watch The Evil Grandmother's barely there lips wrap greasy around a fast-food cup straw, listen to her complain about the "peon food" so fiercely that bits of French fry shot from her mouth with a flat splat on the dashboard, tales of Julia's misery told with the covers up to our chins in the dark, causing me to howl and twist with guilt. I'd never stop feeling bad about it.

Julia always told me stories this way: her cheeks washed in the cool glow of moonlight, she trapped her whispers between two cupped hands against my head and I would get to see up close how perfect her ears were, imagine that spot just behind the lobe as soft as a bud. She taught me everything I know about us this way.

She explained to me that my memories were implants. Formed by years and years of listening to the telling and retelling of stories about me (*Easter where on earth did you ever get that word anyway?),* the stories becoming virile little tadpoles, squiggling their way into the folds of my brain (*I remember the teacher told me that you were the youngest kid she'd ever known to make a racial slur).* These implants made themselves indistinguishable from the real memories (*I'm sure you didn't know what it meant. My god, can you imagine how embarrassing?)* My "memories."

There are some I generated myself, because I was there and I saw it and I knew for sure. I remembered pouring five or six Pixie Sticks onto a plate and then lapping up the tiny pyramid of sugar like a dog. The Evil Grandmother thought it was disgusting, which made me like it even more. I sneezed in threes and caught the chicken pox so bad that blisters were erupting in my mouth and underneath my eyelids. I remember hearing The Father fall down the stairs, the sound of him yelping when he broke his ankle. I remember the first time I touched his scar, all purple and angry and hard and raised; there was bounce to it, unlike normal skin, spongy and resistant. I felt it whenever he'd let me.

But the idea of these pesky little tadpole memories, disguised, hiding, polluting my brain, made me feel unsure of everything. I really should have tagged them before they wriggled in, snapped a serialized marker onto their tails. Or draped them in bells so they would unwittingly announce themselves as fakes, but I didn't think of it then. I was too young.

So Julia tried to help me see what was real and what was fake. She told me that there were ways of distinguishing and that she always knew for sure. You see, Julia had a special talent with brains. She could tell right away if a memory was an implant. She could even tell me who'd implanted it. She said that she had this special ability because she was sort of like a memory herself, squiggling her way through the folds of my brain with the rest of them and drawing out the fakes. Julia the Memory. She said that, just like a regular memory, she worked to serve me, help me make sense of myself in the world. But I had to laugh at that; nod my head of course, but on the inside laugh and disagree. Because Julia was the *reason* I didn't make sense in the world. And we always did everything she wanted to do.

The Tooth House—
Pulp and Stories

The Tooth House. Our house. Named so (by me) for its remarkable resemblance to a tooth. It struck me so when I first looked in the secret anatomy book I found in The Grandmother's basement. A picture of a tooth, bisected like a deviled egg, all of its layers nicely exposed. I learned that teeth have pulp. Soft, soggy centers. In the drawing the pulp was yellow and stitched with red and blue veins, which I dragged my fingers along until they wound together so tight that I couldn't be sure which vein had belonged to which finger.

The outside part of the tooth was white—a helmet of hard enamel, grizzled by all of the stuff you put in your mouth, eroded and chipped and rotted to the pulp in concentrated black whorls when you eat too much candy. Which was a bad habit of Julia's. Always eating too much candy, though she never had a cavity. I'd had about four so far and the dentist told me that, while disappointing, it was still conservative compared to some. I told him that Julia ate way more candy than I did and he said, "Who?" and raised his eyebrows up at The Mother who always used to come into the room with me for some reason and smile with her chin down the way I watched her do it in mirrors when she thought she was alone. The doctor's forehead looked like a package of uncooked sausages when he raised his eyebrows like that. So squishy and unattractive. I looked over at The Mother and she twisted her sweatshirt in her hands and smiled harder with her chin down.

Whenever I thought about that anatomy book, and that pulpy tooth in the picture, I suctioned my tongue over my teeth like a mouth guard.

Pulp.

Pulp inside teeth.

The most succulent section of a fleshy fruit; the fibrous inside of a spleen; a word to describe the parts of things that rot first. How could there be something so delicate in a tooth? Teeth that were made for gnashing and chewing and shredding. Or ripping unruly plastic tags from clothes when The Mother wasn't looking so she couldn't say,

> "Do you have any idea how much those teeth cost, Easter? Do you want to pay for the dental work when you crack one?"

I'd even hoped to one day use my teeth to twist the cap off a beer bottle in a dark bar. Someone tries to pick a fight with me; bumps into me purposefully or something like that. Makes mention of how ugly I am loud enough for me to hear. I mutter something quietly without looking up and the anchor-tattooed forearm of a worn-looking bartender emerges from a shadow with my beer in hand. I bring it to my mouth and snap it open using just my teeth. The grunty foe is duly intimidated. I resume my quiet, thoughtful drinking.

That's just the fantasy, though; something I picked up from watching old movies at night. The reality is much grimmer: While maintaining confrontational eye contact, Easter attempts to bite off the cap. Her teeth break suddenly, the sound unfathomable, and all of her pulp gushes out onto the floor. The grunty foe, not even remotely intimidated, proceeds to beat the crap out of her while she writhes on the ground with her hand over her mouth, scraping frantic streaks into her own thick pulp with the heels of her boots.

Stupid, pulpy teeth. Destroying my dream.

I'd actually had a similar concern about glasses a few years ago when The Mother took me to see an eye doctor. She thought that I wasn't seeing things in a normal way.

Eyeglasses and teeth: both breakable, valuable things that you have to carry with you *all* the time. Hanging there precariously like earrings without backings, threatening to

fall out, chip off, crack to the quick because of some innocent nut or seed or beer bottle.

With my tongue suctioned to my teeth, I realized that if
our cul-de-sac were a jaw, The House would be a canine.
Not only because of where it was placed with respect to
the other houses (nestled toward the back of the cres-
cent, which would technically be the *front* of the mouth,
between a white-slatted spread of incisors and a squat
molar where The Parents moved the car at night), but
also because of its shape. The House was taller than the
other houses and seemed to lean backward into its dark
gray roof, which was badly in need of retiling. I'm not sure
if The House was actually leaning or if it was just so tall
that it sort of appeared that way from my much lower per-
spective. To me, it looked like an interrupted stretch. The
whole thing twisted with dissatisfaction. White siding up
and down like rippled enamel. Swollen gums gathered at
the bottom in the form of big-berried bushes. Wide black
cavities, our basement windows, peeking over the top.

The Parents were very careful not to let any of our pulp spill
out into the yard.

The only things that did manage to escape were corkscrews
of smoke from a cracked-open basement cavity. It was from
this cavity that The Father blew the evidence of his remain-
ing relationship with smoking. He was supposed to have
quit years ago and told The Mother that he had, but that the
residual effect of being a life-long smoker was continuing to

smoke. Which didn't make any sense to me, but which she would laugh at. That kind of "I give up" laugh in which she shakes her head to the quiet tune of her disapproval.

On still nights, the smoke would lie over the grass for a moment before it disappeared.

The way that Julia lay there once, grass peeking in bundles from between her white fingers, one blade against her open eye. She'd fallen from the roof trying to retrieve our neon plastic boomerang, which she clutched in her hand, spattered in the blood that had escaped with the bone which erupted from her twisted neck.

Julia died a lot.

The Terrible Thing

This morning was my first visit to The Tooth House in weeks. And technically a scheduled visit, stickered onto my calendar hanging on the June Room wall, each Sunday staring at me like a peek of someone's skin between buttons. Irresistible to look at, yet to look made me feel so guilty. The Mother had become too depressing. I wanted to stab her, impale her eyeballs onto a barbeque fork and roast them like marshmallows till they popped. She'd gone all flat, a paper doll flapping in the wind, so weak and boring and barely there. But she still smelled like her old full self, which made me feel bad about wanting to skewer her eyeballs. The Father was the exact same because he never changed.

I'm starting to think that it was The Terrible Thing itself that roused me from sleep this morning. The Terrible Thing that fought the sleep drugs and dragged me to The House and up the stairs to the bathroom that no longer smelled like powder and bath oil but cold and metallic and not like The Mother at all.

But that's impossible. The Terrible Thing couldn't have woken me up. It was most likely the dread of having to face the girls from the Craft Room last night. Dread so powerful that it shook me from the inside out.

I wonder if Julia found it yet.

I really had no idea if she was coming back for me or not. A big part of me felt as though she wouldn't. Probably because she'd dropped a boulder on me. Which seems like a pretty clear sign. Like I said, Julia could be scary when she was mad. And leaving her in The Woods to die alone was probably one of those things she would call "unacceptable." Like people who offend easily and funky eyeglasses and the way The Mother ate salad.

Hopefully she'd find The Terrible Thing more than unacceptable, but I don't know if she would. She might find it perfectly acceptable. And I don't know how I'd be able to disagree. Because in a way I found it perfectly acceptable as well. Almost expected.

The irregular wind moved the leaves far above my face, their waxy exteriors reflecting the sun as erratically as a wave making its way to shore. Tiny pockets of concentrated brightness here and there. They twittered purposefully, as though they might be trying to pass me a whispered message. I listened closely but couldn't make anything out.

It was time for me to resume the lesson I started teaching myself this morning. The lesson I had to learn before I saw Lev again. The long-necked Lev, still as a reptile, watching behind white film. Watching for me to betray that I wasn't actually wonderful. That I didn't know how to smoke like a professional addict. That I'd faked it that time in the Miniature Wonderland parking lot. That I was a liar. Which I am.

We'd stood, Lev and I, legs together, shoulders up, tucking ourselves in against the cold the way that people do when they're just standing there outside, exposed. I didn't like the idea of Lev exposed to the elements; the idea of his thin skin wind-whipped, his delicate eyes watering. He lit a cigarette and handed it to me and I took it without thinking, held it with fingers splayed idiotically like a reaching tree frog. Real smoker's fingers aren't scared of the burning embers; their fingers coexist with it. Mine were terrified and it showed.

"Do you smoke?" he asked, clearly noticing.
"Oh yeah," I said, painfully aware of the fact that if someone actually smoked, they wouldn't say "oh yeah" like that. They'd treat it like a curse, an inconvenience, a burden that they'd taken on and now had to deal with.

I proceeded to slurp squirrely puffs from the yellow end like a first-class ass, and the long-necked Lev was gentlemanly enough not to say anything. Instead he told me that basketballs felt like chicken skin under his fingers and asked me if I preferred to hang upside-down from my legs or right-side-up from my arms. And we talked about the

Miniature Wonderland and he asked me if I'd ever had a boyfriend before. Obviously I lied.

Thankfully I still had access to my pockets beneath the rock, so I reached in. The very bottoms were soaked in blood. I pulverized a tiny clot of gore with my thumb and index finger through the fabric and remembered the time Julia died of the flesh-eating disease.

I removed my lighter and a cigarette. And lay there inhaling deeper and deeper lungfuls, mimicking every smoking technique I'd ever seen as I watched the leaves move like waves and make the sound of rice falling into a metal pot on a hot stove. In the kitchen, where I wished very badly to see The Mother at six o'clock tonight.

The tops of my pinched thighs looked bloated and purple and shiny. I grazed one with my fingers and couldn't feel it at all. I think they call this muscle death or acute paralysis or good old-fashioned instant amputation. Either way, they looked cool. Like a pair of big fat sucked-on cigars. It's a good thing I wore shorts today otherwise I might not have been able to see them.

I couldn't help but wonder what my body would look like when it was eventually found. I think what I'll probably do, when it starts to feel like I'm really going to die, is arrange myself into a position a bit more damsel-y and attractive. Less clumsy. Because a bloody, broken, smashed-up girl is attractive to people. Scuff of dirt on the cheek, accentuating the bone; blood falling over a plump lower lip, exaggerating the pout; deep red bringing out the color of the eyes; hair volumized with trauma. They'll wonder, what happened to this troubled girl? This girl with all of those beautiful troubles. Because a girl's troubles aren't actually troubles but accessories. What could my lovely troubles have been? What had I blown so adorably out of proportion? I wish that I'd mastered the abuse aesthetic before having this rock land on me. But who could have known, right? I guess I should have. Julia has been crush-me-with-a-rock angry over far less.

I wish that I really were all troubled and beautiful the way that some people are. Give myself the kind of beginning worthy of the Biography Channel. Being crushed by a rock is too dramatic an end for a story that begins with being born in Canada. Here's my real Biography beginning:

Easter was born an orphan. You might think that no one can be born an orphan because you have to at least have a mother to be born, but Easter always had the distinct feeling that her mother was already dead when she (Easter) gouged her way into the world. The other condition that allows one to be born an orphan, and this was also true of Easter, is if no one knows exactly where you were born, or how you were born. If you just appear one day in a wicker basket on the steps of a tooth-shaped house like Easter did, you're an orphan and born that way.

The Tooth House sat snugly in a cul-de-sac at the edge of a field that would eventually contain another cul-de-sac, a mirror copy of the first. But The Mother and The Father didn't know that yet. And Easter didn't even know what a cul-de-sac was. What she did know was that she was terribly uncomfortable. The discomfort was coldness, though of course she didn't realize it. All she could do was cry about it, take in short, harsh breaths and shoot out high-pitched squeals.

The Mother and The Father didn't notice at first because they were sizzling bacon and eggs on the stove that morning for breakfast. The volcanic bubbling of everything in one pan made it very difficult to hear a crying child on the doorstep.

Anyway, that is where Easter sat until finally Julia opened the door, her hair wet and dripping and thick as dreadlocks and a yellow towel tied tight around her chest. Julia had been taking her first bath alone while The Parents cooked breakfast, which is why the smell of bacon always made her feel dirty. She glided her bare bum across the slick bottom of the tub, creating giant waves that sucked up the army men she'd perched precariously around the porcelain perimeter. The water was red with casualties, or perhaps it was the marker she'd used to draw wounds on the toys and her own soft body. She'd been chanting in her head, "Don't drown, don't drown, don't drown, otherwise you'll never be allowed to do this again." And it must have worked because she didn't drown but lived to find Easter on the doorstep. Lived even to scoop her up and stop her crying and tuck her into a warm doll crib.

Julia took care of Easter for the first little while in secret, came up with excuses for mashing up food and bringing it upstairs, and snuck loads of laundry into the wash after The Parents went to bed. When she finally told The Parents about her little project, they made room for it and told Julia that she could name it. She chose the name Easter because that's what day it was when she found the little thing.

That's actually how it happened. None of this Niagara Falls and traumatic car rides with The Evil Grandmother and freezing cold water splashing up between the Maid of the Mist boat rails, coming together and confusing itself with my persistent knocking on the world's warm, wet double doors.

The Mother

Phyllis the Evil Grandmother is a fucking bitch, and when I first realized that Phyllis was a fucking bitch, I also realized that the poor Mother was someone's daughter. And not just anyone's daughter but a fucking bitch's daughter.

Phyllis the Fucking Bitch always wore some manifestation of "expensive lady suit" no matter what season it was. If it was winter, she would wear a dark, woolly skirt and blazer, thick nylons, and heaps of heavy silver jewelry fastened around her wrists and neck like a pillory. Inside the house, black leather boots became a pair of embroidered slippers. Phyllis's feet never spent more than a few seconds unshackled.

In summer she wore light, flowing pant suits, maybe in a coral or light blue color, and was swimming in gold necklaces with big, shining ornaments pulling on her ears like a pair of anvils. Tan leather sandals transformed into a pair of sheer footies in the house.

And she didn't move often. She greatly preferred to ask other people to move for her, follow her bellowed instructions from the porch while you mixed her cocktail in the kitchen: tomato juice and vodka, which shuddered when passed into her hands. She had no shame when it came to asking for small favors. I think if it were physically possible, she would have asked someone to go to the bathroom for her.

Though The Mother looked a lot like her, Phyllis the Fucking Bitch always insisted that she got her father's "baboonish eyebrows" or his "strong, masculine nose." On Sunday afternoons she "treated" The Mother, Julia, and me to brunch at the club where she used to golf a long, long time ago. It was always a stressful affair during which Phyllis would watch our hands as we reached for bread from the basket at the center of the table, or follow our too-full forks from our plates to our mouths. She was never *not* looking when Julia or I spilled something, or accidentally allowed food to fall from our nervous lips as we chewed. She could sense a mistake even before it happened, or perhaps she caused them with her accusatory eyes.

By the time that we left the restaurant and made it back to the safety of our car, The Mother always looked a bit crumpled. We would attempt to revive her from the backseat. Tell her that Phyllis the Fucking Bitch was an old drunk, that she was just jealous of The Mother for growing up to be so beautiful and have such excellent kids.

The Mother would laugh and thank me, then scold me for

talking about The Grandmother that way, but that was just a formality. You could see that it soothed her to hear that we were unaffected by Phyllis the Fucking Bitch.

The Mother didn't remember much about her father. Just his feet one summer afternoon: shapely leather shoes, red-brown, and beautifully arranged on the grass. Though she was old enough to walk, she crawled on hands and knees over to his feet and he fed her an olive from his martini, then patted her head as though she really were the dog she was pretending to be.

He died shortly after, in a bad car accident. Phyllis had always told The Mother that the reason he went careening into a wide cement pole at fifty miles an hour was because he was getting his penis sucked on by the widow next door and lost control of the car.

Phyllis told her that, as soon as they hit the pole, the widow's jaws clamped shut and bit his penis off, a reflex in response to the crash. They found it in her mouth the next morning when the mortician pried her jaws open.

I always wondered if Phyllis kept it somewhere, in a jar, maybe, at the back of her closet. Or maybe it was in something more official-looking. Some hazardous waste bag that the doctors placed it in with tweezers and a gloved hand. I bet it looks more like a fig now, all purple and dried up. Or maybe she had it preserved and vacuum-sealed. I imagined it withering in the widow's mouth overnight so many years ago, covering her chin in dick blood. Dick blood beard, dick blood beard. Try saying that five times fast. Actually, try saying "five times fast" five times fast.

Phyllis was as full of lies as I was, but somehow she wasn't embarrassed by them. She told them openly, without shame. Mixed them right up with all of the true stuff she said, so it was very hard to tell which was which. That's why The Mother really had no idea if she should believe this story or not and, over the years, grew too scared to try to actually find out. Instead, she kept the broad-shouldered saint in her head. The generous king who kept her secrets, retrieved her balls, fed her cake. Wise beyond his years, a comfort to the sick and savior of the weak. The Mother must have seen some of these same qualities in The Father way back when, but thinking of him now, it doesn't seem possible.

Phyllis's social life became quite active after her husband died. She went to parties where live bands shook like it was Gatsby's house and people had fancy hats to go with their fancy outfits. In the same closet where she might have kept Grandpa's dick, Phyllis had an enormous wardrobe of gowns draped in mauve plastic protectors with clear little windows over the hearts so you could see what was inside. Julia and I went over once to help her organize the closet, move the body bags from one rack to another. It was while we were moving summer clothes to the off-season rack that she told us a few things about our grandfather. She enjoyed letting us know the reasons why her life was harder than anyone else's.

She said that she hated him.

That he was a podiatrist.

And whenever they went out, no one wanted to shake his footy hand. They did so reluctantly, out of politeness, but she always saw them afterward, casually wiping their palms on napkins or their suit jackets. Every time he opened his mouth she wanted to strangle him. Berate him in front of the others so that they knew she was better than he was. And that she knew it too.

She said that he had a hunched back from kneeling at people's feet all day while they watched the bald spot on the crown of his head expand over the years, and that she was a perfect masterpiece of genetics and good taste. Disappointment swirled around her like cigar smoke. Obscuring her eyes and the sharp corners of her thin body, making her seem softer and more attractive than she really was.

Before she was completely consumed by all of the whirling disappointment, she changed the subject with an order about how she wanted her afternoon suits organized.

Easter Story

One morning a bell rang from downstairs in such a strange and ferocious way that it woke Easter right up. She could tell from the light through her curtains that she'd slept in later than usual, which made sense considering the fact that she blew right through bedtime last night watching movies on the couch alone, secretly, while everyone else was asleep.

She'd watched a movie about a girl who woke up one morning beneath different sheets in a different bed in a different room in a different house, with a different family carrying out a most unfamiliar morning shuffle downstairs. Her whole life before that moment might have been a dream, a very real dream, but now she was waking up to her actual life. Easter dragged a hand along her face to see if the same thing had happened to her. Same face, same sleep smell between the sheets. She could feel the familiarity as plainly as a burn.

That bell was very different, though. Not only unique to her *regular mornings, but also a strange way for a bell to sound. It didn't sound like it was in someone's hand, a wrist shaking ever so slightly, the sound of the bell filling the air like incense from a thurible, but rather this bell was being banged against something hard. Back and forth and back and forth and back and forth.*

She walked to the stairs in socked feet, avoiding the creaks in the hardwood known well to her and even better to Julia. She sat slowly down on the middle step and peeked through the vertical dowels beneath the banister, her arms and feet all tucked in the way she imagined a spy's would be if they were peeking in on someone.

The Mother appeared to have attached a bell to the basement doorframe and was now testing it vigorously, bringing the door back and forth and back and forth and back and forth so that it sounded more like a gong than a bell. Her hair looked sweaty, her head warm, and Easter thought about the way The Mother never touched her face with her hands. She was all forearm and wrist when it came to daubing up beads of sweat and swiping hair from her face.

She always did the same for Easter, too; no hands on the face, just soft inner wrists and arms because, as Easter knew very well, The Mother believed that touching your face would cause unsightly blemishes to sprout. And The Mother didn't want Easter to have unsightly blemishes just as much as she didn't want herself to have unsightly blemishes, because Easter knew that The Mother wanted only good things for her and loved her more than she loved herself. Wanted her as beautiful and happy and perfect as she could be, even though she was very bad at making Easter feel beautiful and happy and perfect.

Easter sometimes felt like a cherished heirloom, a vase sitting in the middle of the table, there but not really there, kept clean and filled with lovely living flowers, watered and tended to, but also ignored. Listening and seeing everything in secret.

Easter watched. The Mother struggled with the nails lying on the floor. They rolled along the circular path set out by the size of their heads, little synchronized swimmers evading her grasp. She wore a long white T-shirt and jeans. Easter knew they were her most "hard working" jeans. And when The Mother got up for a glass of water, Easter noticed that she'd even tied her running shoes extra tight in readiness for a morning all full of physical labor.

Easter knew The Mother so well. Knew everything she'd do and say before she did and said it. Because The Mother had passed The Lonely along to Easter, the same Lonely but different because it had moved, contracted differently: the way a secret whispered into ears and through mouths mutates; a disease from genome to genome.

The Mother returned to the doorframe and began testing the bell again. Easter rose from the stairs and approached her with her hands over her ears.

"What are you doing?" she yelled.

The Mother suddenly stopped and Easter saw beads of sweat

on her upper lip. She daubed them delicately in her soft, wristly way, her eyes red-rimmed and wide.

> "Oh hello, honey. I'm putting bells on the doors."
> "Why?"
> "Well, you know, I'm tired of not knowing where you people are all the time."
> "So you're putting bells on the doors?"
> "That's right."
> "So you know where we are."
> "Yes dear."
> "Like a jingly collar?"
> "What's that?" Her voice hit a skip somewhere in the middle.
> "Like a jingly collar on a cat."

Her eyes grew even wider and she might have nodded a bit, but it was hard to tell. She turned around again and resumed banging the bell against the door.

Easter turned around and thought about bells on collars. What those bells might do to a person or a cat, jingling all the time, some times more than others. She pulled a bowl from the cupboard, a spoon from the drawer.

And then she banged them together to get The Mother's attention again. The Mother jumped and landed on a couple of her tiny rolling nails. Easter imagined them squishing like bugs.

> "Easter! What is it?"
> "Well, I was just getting my cereal here and had a question."

"Okay."
"Are you going to install those on every door?"
"Every door."
"Even my door?"
"Even your door, Easter."
"I don't know if I like that."
"How come, honey?"
"I don't know."

The Mother frowned and gave Easter a kiss on the cheek.

Easter vowed then in her head to never attach a bell to an animal's collar, because she decided that hearing a bell all the time, every time you did something, loud around your neck near your ears, keeping you from doing things that you wanted to do, forcing you to do things you didn't, making you like certain things not because you really liked them but because they wouldn't make the sound of the bell, or like them because they would make the sound of the bell, would be just awful.

The Mother, with bells inflating her pockets now, proceeded to pinch the little nails from the floor and into her palm and make her way up the stairs to start on the bedrooms (she also managed give Easter another kiss, this time on the forehead). Easter promptly wiped the kiss off and moved to the fridge to get the milk for her cereal.

And the bell rang often. So often that she'd even stopped noticing. So often that instead of waking her up, the bells simply tucked themselves neatly into her dreams and in the morning she had no memory of their ringing at all.

The Tooth house—Bathroom

Cold against my cheek, my breath showed itself on the mirror. Because sometimes I put my face against it. The side of my face. So my eyelashes swept and folded as I blinked. My nostrils puffed smaller prints of breath on the mirror, a glimpse into the world of things not seen, like water splashed against the invisible man. I'm not sure why I did this, but I did. The bathroom was the place to do strange, socially unacceptable things. And I think that pushing your face up hard against the mirror would be as socially unacceptable in a public bathroom as not closing the door to take a crap. So I did it in the bathroom, and not in my bedroom or the hallway or the living room or the kitchen.

The bathroom. Small and white and sanitary.

A tub, occupied for hours by The Mother on Sunday nights.

A toilet over which I'd once found a dead Julia, her pressed-against-the-seat-cheek prying open already-gray lips, peeking tongue still pink, one arm stiff and planked over the open bowl as though she were trying to hide what was inside, bare legs tucked neatly so that her snow-white toes made a string of pearls beneath her.

A sink that Julia had once spit bits of teeth into for weeks for no good reason, then choked on one night in her sleep, coughing white puffs of powder-pulverized tooth into the air while I watched, helpless, next to her in bed.

She'd been dying like this, over and over again since we were young. Or I was young. I don't remember Julia ever being as young as I was the first time I watched her die. Crushed to death by the contents Phyllis's basement.

Across from the toilet and the sink: a little chest of drawers with no rhyme or reason. Half-empty tubes of things rarely used mingled with loose, gifted bath beads. Snapped elastics moved like trapped worms when you picked them up. Bobby pins in every size; worn, thumb-smudged business cards; for a while a plastic knife and fork.

And between the toilet and chest of drawers: me, sitting with my legs crossed in front of the mirror, which hung from the door. I moved my face back, off the mirror, and examined what I'd left behind. Wetness. Recent. A few moments ago an oyster was sucked from its shell and now that shell looked the same as what I'd left on this mirror.

What I saw as I pulled my face back was as terrible and disgusting as an oyster.

Because my name is Easter and I have a terrible and disgusting face.

It really is the most terrible and disgusting face. Even if I tried my hardest I couldn't come up with a more frustrating set of features. Every little thing about it is just the tiniest bit off. I don't have any glaringly obvious issues like a huge birthmark or sideburns or a witch nose, but I would almost prefer something like that to the collection of irritating little problems that make up this *thing* I have to put between myself and the world.

My nose is exactly three millimeters too wide for my face. Either that or the little marble end of my nose is too small, which makes my nostrils just too bulbous, like I stuffed invisible wine corks in them or something. It's really hard to tell without a second opinion. Which I would never ask for. I wouldn't want people to think that I cared so much.

I have about thirty too many freckles. In other words, just enough for it to stop being cute.

My forehead is roughly half an inch too long, and it gives my whole face the bottom-heavy look of a soaking wet wool coat. Picture a too-freckly Richard Nixon with long brown hair. But uglier. There you go. That's me. My face is also about an inch too wide, and when I stare at myself for a *really* long time, I stop looking human. The way that a word starts to seem unreal as you repeat it, my face unravels.

My mouth is all right, but still suffering from some decidedly unfixable flaws. At first you might think that the main problem is that it's too wide, and of course you would be right. My mouth is quite easily too wide for my face. When I smile it extends even past my horribly round eyes. But that isn't the real issue, and it was only after years of examination that I realized what the actual problem was. It's that my Cupid's bow is less of a little dip and more of a greedy scoop.

My jaw is wide, but my chin is small, and it makes my whole head look like there is far too much face occupying it. Which is of course exaggerated by the fact that my head is the size and shape of an overripe picnic watermelon. At first glance I probably just look like a face with legs.

My eyes are a serious problem too. The shape of golf balls and a dull greeny blue. Like the Alkylphenol River, a small body of water named after the most concentrated chemical compound found within it, or perhaps the name of the native tribe that originally lived around there. I can never remember. Either way, these eyes are the color of someone who has frozen to death. In the Alkylphenol River. And was finally found, weeks later, with the spring thaw.

So that's what I'm working with in this world. My face, like a bad logo, holding me back from being as successful, or in this case as happy, as I knew I could be.

Five Days with Phyllis the Fucking Bitch

The first time we ever went to Phyllis's house, we had to stay there for five whole days. If we'd had a friend we could have stayed at her house, said The Father when I wouldn't stop crying about it. I remember the house looked surprisingly ticklish. Surprising because it was strange that a house should look ticklish at all, but also because Phyllis was such a nasty old bitch that I couldn't imagine the house had any reason to feel tickled.

We expected it to be yellow and brown and rotting: bricks like dead teeth, floors weak as wet toilet paper, amnion of dust wrapping up every chair and carpet and cutting board.

But it turned out that wasn't the case. There were no bricks at all but clean blue panels that rippled along the sides. A narrow wrap-around porch grabbed around the middle like a one-armed hug. And succulents, a wadded mass of succulents, billowing from dark soil against the covered section of the porch. The front lawn glowed like a million test tubes of radioactive goo.

She would sit on her porch and watch people admire the lawn as they passed by. Her legs crossed at the ankles, appearing smooth and mercifully unscathed by veins beneath the ruse of the too-tan nylons she clipped to some unimaginable device beneath her skirt. She seemed to have an endlessly refreshed supply of those too-tan nylons. A smartly pressed white shirt too unbuttoned, her hair up and sprayed stiff like a character from Clue.

Periodically she would stand up, remove the cushion from her seat, and use it to protect her nylons from the concrete when she kneeled down and examined her blades of grass, which were as straight and erect as the hair on a soldier's head.

When we first approached her, she was waiting for us on the porch. I was hanging off The Mother's arm, my small red suitcase bouncing behind me, chipping into the edge of her army of green-haired soldiers. She stood up suddenly, the teacup in her lap tumbling down the front of her skirt and performing a loud pirouette on the porch before it came to a complete stop.

> "Easter, for god's sake, would you quit dragging that bag? Lift it, girl, use your arms! You're going to gouge a hole in my lawn!"

The Mother stopped abruptly and picked up my bag with her other arm. I clung to her tighter.

"You should let her do that herself." Phyllis picked up the teacup from the porch as she continued. "She's got two working arms, doesn't she?" She placed the teacup on a small round table next to her chair. "She knows what to do."

Then she pulled an eyebrow up ever so slightly.

For Phyllis to even attempt to move an eyebrow indicated a depth of seriousness I'd not yet encountered. The Mother seemed to swallow the last millisecond of time on earth, reversing it, like how a videotape jerks backward when it's paused. The suitcase was suddenly back in my hand again and The Mother spoke to me through a forced smile: "Be careful, honey." We started to walk again. I did my best to control the hair-trigger plastic wheels but it was hard.

"Sorry, Mom. Did you stain your skirt?"

The Mother was always apologizing to Phyllis the Fucking Bitch.

"No, I don't think so," Phyllis replied.

And she got a funny look on her face, like The Mother should have known that already. Phyllis never stains her clothes because all she consumes after two o'clock p.m. is hamster-sized sips of vodka.

"Well, sorry anyway."
"It's fine, dear."

All the while I'd been pulling my unpredictable suitcase as

slowly as possible, trying my best not to touch Phyllis's lawn, the flat green beast seeming to snarl at me whenever I moved too close for comfort. Tiny steps, as slowly as possible, inch by inch, wormlike, the sound of the wheels thundered like an old engine idling.

Phyllis and The Mother watched silently with widening eyes until The Mother gave my arm a little tug and laughed nervously and said, "Come on, dear, we haven't got all day." But I couldn't make myself go any faster. I had to be as careful as possible.

The Mother, forcing laughter, grabbed my suitcase again and pulled me up to the steps quickly. Then she said to Phyllis,

> "So we'll be back on Friday night."
> "I know, I know, you've told me a thousand times now, dear. It's not like I'm going to forget an event that I'll likely be looking forward to in half an hour."
> "Don't talk like that, Mom. She's not going to bug you. And you can just let her do whatever she wants, okay? She's not the kind of kid to take advantage."
> "I know. She's a very good girl. Go."
> "All right."

The Mother squatted down, my fingers still suctioned to her cool white arm.

> "Easter. Let go."

I let go of her and a fat tear rolled down my cheek.

"What's the matter, Easter? It better not be that you have to stay with your grandmother, because if it is, I think I'm going to lose it."

"You can't *leave* me with her, Mom. You can't. She hates me."

I tried to control my volume so that Phyllis couldn't hear, but the tears made it very difficult, forcing my voice up into shrillness as unpredictably as my suitcase moved over the bumpy walkway.

The Mother stroked the hair from my hot face and held it behind me in a ponytail. Let cool air onto the back of my neck and through perfectly puckered lips blew a stream of chilled breath over my face, bringing creaminess back into the angry red blotches. She said,

"Look, I'm sorry, Easter. She doesn't hate you. She's just not good at making you think otherwise. I know this might seem awful right now, but I promise the next five days will fly by. And when we get back, we'll buy you something. Whatever you want."

"A dog?" I asked in my hissy whisper.

"Anything but a dog."

"A pool?"

"Anything but a dog or a pool."

I crossed my arms and entered hot-face-first into a full-on skulk. The Mother stood up, kissed the top of my head, and trotted to the car. She reached over The Father and gave the horn two cheerful honks and they motored quickly down the street and out of sight. Phyllis the Fucking Bitch walked up behind me and her shadow swallowed me whole.

The sound of a screen door creaking caused us both to look up and see Phyllis's neighbor emerge from his front door. He wore a blue shirt with a stiff collar and his hands had a thin, lettuce-like quality to them that made me feel queasy. The sun bounced off his bald head and his steadily darkening transition lenses. Short, wired frame and a mouth that moved as slightly as a sphincter.

"Hello, Phyllis! Who've you got there?" blew out of his mouth.

I imagined his breath and suppressed a gag.

"Hello, Norman. This is my granddaughter. Her name is Easter, don't ask me why."

Norman didn't seem to notice Phyllis's unnecessary jab at a helpless kid. He kept his eyes on her and smiled. It was mostly gum. Weak-looking teeth sprouted like an afterthought at the bottom.

"Hello, Easter."
"Hi," I mumbled.

I looked up at Phyllis to indicate that we should make our escape into the house but she was leaned over backward, her skirt pulled up high as she fiddled with a run in the thigh of her nylons. Or perhaps that unimaginable device that held them up had malfunctioned. Norman was watching her hungrily, lowering both of his crisp hands into his pockets and bringing his bottom lip up over the top one, over and over again in a slow unconscious way.

"Have you been using any of that fertilizer, Phyllis?" he finally hollered, moving his fingers around behind the pleats of his khakis.

The sound of her name broke Phyllis from that momentary fascination with her snagged nylons.

"What's that, Norman?"

"I was just wondering if you'd used any of my fertilizer yet?" he repeated anxiously.

"Oh, no, Norman. I think I'm doing just fine without your fertilizer. But thanks for leaving it in my sun porch. It was lovely to walk in to the smell of hot shit that morning."

Norman's smile transformed into a frown. His hands stopped moving.

"Oh," he said, "right. Well, I'm sorry, but it looked like your lawn could use the nourishment."

He removed his hands from his pockets and stood stiff-armed and foolish-feeling. Phyllis let the last drops of unspilled vodka slide into her mouth from the teacup and then herded me with the back of her hand up the walk, onto her porch, and through the front door.

"Goodbye, Norman," she replied just before the screen closed shut.

The inside of her house looked like the inside of any other house, except that it smelled like an old silverware drawer and there seemed to be an inexplicable breeze trapped inside, fondling the tassels on the pillows in the living room and squeezing the slightest tinkling sound from between the champagne-colored crystals on a chandelier that hung in the foyer. I don't think that Phyllis noticed the breeze anymore. It swirled around her, bounced off her decorative plates, wove around the banister, all without her so much as batting an eyelash.

Her floors were nothing like wet toilet paper. They were hardwood with a perfectly shaped red rug running through every hallway and up the stairs and expanding to cover each room except for the bedrooms, which contained thick, swampy carpets of various colors that sucked on your feet as you walked.

There wasn't an amnion of dust covering everything up, but I'm sure that it was because it would be impossible for it to settle with that trapped breeze bouncing around all the time like a rambunctious pet.

Phyllis took us up the red-carpet stairs gesturing toward rooms and objects and saying things like "towel cupboard" and "finicky flusher." We started down a long hallway that ended at a brown door. The red carpet was even softer than it looked and impressed beneath my warm, socked feet.

"Well, this is your room. I hope you find it comfortable, dear."

I looked up at her.

"Go ahead, open the door."

So I did.

Inside was a double bed, with a pilled orange blanket on top of it that she'd tucked between the mattress and the box spring so the whole thing looked like a giant shoebox.

A large, cream-colored radiator with diagonal slats in it like a garden fence lined the far wall of the room, and on top of it spread a vast collection of framed photographs, some as big as doormats, others smaller, like the kinds of pictures that people keep in their wallet accordions.

Most of the pictures were of people that we'd never seen before: a pair of men in neat white tuxedos, standing on a cruise ship with life preservers around their necks like leis and short glasses in their hands. Their throats were bloated like a pair of warbling frogs and big smiles distorted their faces. Behind that, a picture of a woman holding together a thick orange coat with one elegantly clasped hand. She had short hair and windblown cheeks that were squeezing her mouth into a sort of straight-across smile. A blurry city behind her. Beside that picture, a man dressed up as a colonial general, complete with oversized elephant gun. A proud-looking pose: one fist on his waist, one foot on a woman dressed up like a tiger. She lay on the floor next to him with a face mocking death, two hands mimicking claws. Purple and black streamers hung behind them while a cauldron-shaped fondue pot bubbled to the right.

And *there* was a picture of The Mother. At the zoo. Her hair was long and her cheeks were pinched with youth and the sun. A fat brown snake hung over her shoulders and she smiled at the camera. In the background you could just make out the fuzzy shapes of other young girls with bashful boyfriends to take their portraits with a snake.

The walls of the room were lined with floral-patterned wallpaper, predominantly green, that had suffered and bubbled from years of damp winters and humid summers. The red-runner carpet became a green carpet in this room and had sucked up our feet to the ankles.

> "Is this all right then?" Phyllis asked.
> "Yeah."

But of course it wasn't. Nothing was going to be all right until I got to go home.

> "Good. Well, I'll be around. I like to sit on the porch most of the time. Think about the ways I could get some poison into Norman's food."

She waited for me to laugh, so I did.

> "All right, dear, dinner is usually at seven or so. But I guess you probably ate before you came."

"Yeah."

"Well, dinner is at seven most nights, anyway."

"Thanks, Grandma."

I think I really was sinking into the floor. Should I tell some-one about this? The carpet was going to eat my knees if I didn't take action and move. So I moved. I turned and sat on the bed, pulling my feet up quick to cross my legs. Phyllis took that as her hint to leave.

"Well, have fun then," she said, and closed the door behind her.

Julia had already made herself comfortable on the other side of our bed.

"You'd think the old bitch could give us each a room. This place is certainly big enough."

"I'm glad I'm not alone."

"You're such a baby Easter."

"I am not, Julia. I know that you're glad, too; you just won't admit it."

Julia rolled over on to her side and I lay down too. The ceil-ing was spackled and little drips hung stiff, in mid-drop, like on the walls of a cave. Itty bitty stalagmites. I closed my eyes and imagined myself to be as still as one of those drops. Stopped in my tracks, flash frozen. Maybe those little drips were still moving but they were just going so slowly that no one could see. Something small inside of them that still crawls forward, that's still as alive as I am. And they live their whole lives in that small-moving something.

Maybe to someone bigger and faster, I'm barely moving. There's someone watching me, thinking that I'm still as a stalagmite, that I'm a figurine, but I'm not. There is something still alive in me. I began to hear the wet, dripping sounds of a cave echoing through the room. Cold, stagnant, shallow breath. Air like a vacuum, anxious to crack. I should really let Phyllis's breeze in here. This cavernous air would be cleared out in no time. But I couldn't move. I was as still as those frozen drips above my head. And before I knew it, I was asleep.

The next morning, Phyllis knocked on our door.

"Breakfast," she coughed.

Julia and I looked at each other solemnly.

Day one.

The round breakfast table was covered in a yellow-and-white-checkered tablecloth, pulled tight around the edges and clipped with special pins that looked like mallard ducks. Phyllis's arms were covered in bracelets and she wore a brown linen shirtdress and a gold belt. She had decorated the table in towers of buttered limp toast and every different kind of jam. There was a pot of coffee percolating on the stove. I was too young yet for that to interest me, but only just. Still at an age in which coffee was just another disgusting odor associated with being a withered, wrung-out adult.

The jams though, that was a different story. There were as many jams as keys on a piano.

> "I hope you like jam."
> "We do."

Phyllis looked up at me quickly, as though I'd startled her. I took a seat and began inspecting the labels on the jam jars.

> "I was wondering, Easter. I want you to do something for me while you're here. Can you do something for me?"
> "Probably."

Phyllis took a long gulp from her glass of tomato juice. She let a dark red moustache attach itself to her top lip for just a second before she lapped it off expertly with her snake tongue.

> "There are some items of value down in the basement that I'm ready to part with but I need some help to dig them out of the mess. Do you think you could help?"

I didn't want to be the one to make the decision for us. I'd wait for Julia. A long moment passed. Phyllis fiddled with one of the mallard ducks clamped to the edge of the table and I stared at the checked tablecloth for so long that each square began to dance.

> "We've got nothing better to do," Julia finally agreed.

So I nodded.

And that's how we ended up in Phyllis's basement.

The Cube

When Phyllis first opened the door, the basement looked like a Magic Eye picture in the Saturday paper. Like we were face-to-face with a wall of matter and only with serious concentration could we see it as an actual space to enter. But nothing ever appeared. Because, truly, the room was so absolutely packed with things that they all fused together, shaped like Play-Doh to almost the exact dimensions of the room.

It was a brick of Phyllis's life, tucked away underground, and she wanted us to sever it and save something, work our way through it, a tumor to be biopsied. There was a sliver of space at the very top of the room, about the height of a baseball bat, and sun filtered in from the bits of window that peeked over the top of the mess up there.

"So, can you get in there and find a few things for me? I have a list."

She held out piece of paper torn from a long, yellow legal pad. It said:

Elizabeth's chloroform mask
Elizabeth's riot gear
Elizabeth's Arabian fly net
Elizabeth's blindfold hood
Elizabeth's spotted body suit
Elizabeth's head protector
Elizabeth's respiratory measurement mask
Elizabeth's equine inhaler
Elizabeth's gas mask
Elizabeth's armor
Elizabeth's bridle

I looked up at Phyllis but she was already in the kitchen, rummaging under the sink for a stepladder.

"You want me to go into this mess?"

"Well, on top of it first," she replied, wiping some dust off a white vinyl stepping stool and placing it next to my feet. "And then you should probably start digging."

I looked at Julia. She shrugged, stepped up onto the ladder, and climbed on top of the solid mass of basement that we were meant to rummage through. So I followed.
Once I was up there, Phyllis spoke again:

"I'll leave the door open so you always know how to get out, all right?"

"Okay. Wait, Grandma, who's Elizabeth?"

"Elizabeth is your mother's horse."

"She has a horse?"

"Had a horse," Phyllis replied.

Then she walked into the kitchen to prepare a Bloody Mary. Just one, to transition from tomato juice morning into vodka afternoon.

"Named *Elizabeth*..." grumbled Julia from somewhere deeper in the basement.

So Julia and I began our expedition. We felt like a pair of archaeologists going through layers of settled earth, counting the years of growth by the things that we found. We tunneled through the stuff, created pockets, rooms where we could stop for a moment and leave items of interest that we retrieved. We made a tunnel to the door so we could enter and exit fairly easily to use the bathroom or grab something to eat. Phyllis left us trays of toast and jam on the breakfast table that afternoon for lunch, along with two glasses of chocolate milk, four water bottles and a box of granola bars. We brought those with us into the first room that we created, which we were calling The Café.

"I wonder how much money antique horse equipment goes for," Julia said while fingering a whole piece of buttered-limp-toast into her mouth.

"I can't believe Mom never told us she had a horse," I said.

"I think if she told us that she had a horse, then we'd expect to get horses."

"I do kind of expect her to buy me a horse now."

"I told you so."

"Or at least a dog."

"Seriously."

We could always hear Phyllis: slippered feet on the rug, screen door opening and closing, her daily routine kept by a tomato-shaped egg timer that seemed to have limitless settings. A crank first thing in the morning before preparing breakfast, the only time that Phyllis would eat a meal all day. A ding at noon to announce lunch, at which time Phyllis would fetch a piece of celery to place in her drink. Another crank, a ding at 3:00. Time to switch to straight vodka. Another crank and a ding at dinner time. Three dings all together to maintain Phyllis's day, pull her from her stillness on the porch as though from a trance. Three dings we could hear from The Cube, letting us know when our lunch would be placed at the door, when it was safe to leave to use the bathroom, when it was time to clock out for the day.

That first night, once we were safely sealed off in our bedroom, Julia expressed some bitterness about our adventures underground.

"I hate that fucking bitch."

I was lying on the green carpet, letting myself get sucked under slowly. One of my nostrils was already submerged and my lips were shut tight to keep any of the carpet from getting into my mouth.

> "Don't you hate her, Easter?"
> "Mmm."
> "I mean, what kind of a terrible grandmother would send kids into that firetrap? We could suffocate in there. Our tunnels could collapse and we could be crushed or starve to death. I can't even imagine what kinds of particles aggravated my lungs today. We're probably going to die now, from some poisonous mold that we inhaled. Our lungs are probably ravaged. Now, if for some reason I wanted to, I could never be an athlete, that stupid fucking bitch. She stole everything from us, do you realize that?"

I hadn't. And I still didn't. Julia could be dramatic.

She'd been lying on the bed all night after dinner, soaking up the moonlight like a cat on a stoop. She got up and leaned two stiff arms onto the radiator, letting them support her body, which she was craning to get a better view of the porch from the window. Phyllis was down there all right. Watching over her lawn, sipping vodka from her teacup.

> "We should do something to the lawn, Easter."

I raised my head out of the carpet to reply:

> "No Julia. Absolutely not. We've got a whole week with that woman."

"So what? What could be worse than what we're already doing? What could she possibly punish us with?"

"No."

"Please, Easter. Why do you always have to be such a stick in the mud?"

"No Julia."

"Please, please"—

"No! No, no, no, no, no. I won't do it, Julia, so just stop. Why do you always want to make things worse? Why do you always have to make us do these awful things? We wouldn't even be staying here if you'd let us have a friend. We'd be at staying at The Friend's house, like a normal girl." I wanted to cry again.

Goddammit. I hate when crying just happens to you. Like when you're being yelled at by someone or you're very nervous, there's a hostile takeover of your face and chest and all of a sudden you're a crying baby.

"Easter, you'd never do anything fun if it weren't for me. You'd never stand up for yourself or fight back. You're always so worried about 'making trouble' and 'acting normal.' We would barely be human if it weren't for me."

"Julia, that isn't true," I replied weakly.

"Well, I suppose that's right. You certainly do all of the crying for us."

"I know you're just mad because I won't let you ruin Phyllis's lawn. You're mad at me so you're trying to hurt my feelings. I know you don't think what you're saying is true."

"Fine. I hate you. I hate you just as much as I hate Phyllis, maybe even more. I hope you drown in The Cube tomorrow, Easter, I really do."

I knew she didn't mean it, really I did, but it hurt my feelings anyway. I lay as still as I possibly could, until the carpet sucked me all the way under.

At first it was hard to breathe green carpet because it didn't feel like real air. It felt thick and itchy like wool or bushes but after a few terrifying seconds I got used to it, and after a few seconds more, I loved it. Better than air. It invaded me like water up your nose or campfire smoke in your face, but in a fantastic way. I took full, deep, delicious breaths and did back flips in the green. It moved me around like hands, scooping me up under my arms, passing me along, over and under, sideways, upside down, all the while filling me up and scraping a little bit of me off with it when I exhaled. I wanted to be sucked up by every colorful carpet in this whole house. I wish there was a pair of hands like this to move me through Phyllis's basement cube. Cube, cube, cube. I wondered if the basement was actually the shape of a cube. It might be. There's really no way to tell when you're inside of it.

Crush

My cigar-butt legs felt like they were filled with lead, and they felt like lead to my fingers, too. So stiff that I could knock on them. I guess muscle death had already occurred. Coincidentally I'd just read all about "crush syndrome" in my anatomy book. Your legs grow hard as wood when the muscles die, and your whole body fills with toxins. Toxins that can stop up your organs and put you in a coma if you don't die from blood loss first. Quite nasty. But not nearly as nasty as dying on a forest floor. Much different from dying in a bathtub, for example.

A forest floor like this one is already all filled with bugs and flies and beetles and things looking to feast on rotting flesh and lay eggs in warm orifices like mine. When you die on a forest floor the maggots get started on you right way, fully formed and hatched within a day, moving through your body in a warm, rolling mass, devouring you with their hooked mouths. And then you fill with gasses and bloat so terribly that you deflate with a wheeze and leak from everywhere and within a week you're home to more generations of flies and beetles and maggots and worms than you've got in your whole family.

It's the smell that attracts the bugs. Essence of Cadaverine. Of Methane. Of Hydrogen Sulphide. These smells billow around you like steam, attracting all of the things that will rip you up and make a bountiful home of your corpse.

In a bathtub, though, things would be different. In a bathtub during that first day it's only the bacteria that were already inside you that eat you, from the inside out, starting in the intestines and making their way slowly. A whole body filled with traitors, parasites that you grew yourself and nourished with your own body, just waiting to eat you up. That's what happens when you die in a bathtub.

And even though I didn't like the idea of all those bugs eating me up, I didn't necessarily want Julia to come back for me yet either. It was very nice to lie under the rock and smoke those Red Baron cigarettes and watch the living leaves. I thought of Lev's eyes, donut holes dipped in sugary glaze, suddenly standing over me. He would roll the rock off, blow life back into my legs somehow, and we'd walk off down the path, smoking and talking. I'd ask him why it took him so long to come and get me. He'd tell me that he had to wait until the sun was well blocked by leaves, because it singed his skin like poultry in the oven, bits of it coming off like dried petals. And then he'd invite me to live with him underground, with the rest of the subterranean humanoids. And it would be all dark so none of us would have to look at each other, just feel each other, and I knew I felt better than I looked so I'd enthusiastically agree and we'd live together underground happily ever after; I'd lick the glaze from his eyes as the scene faded to black and then you'd never hear from us again. A perfect rescue.

But of course he didn't really live underground. He just looked that way. Really he lived on Princess Street, in a basement bedroom crawling with bugs, bugs that he sometimes accidentally carried out into the world with him, one that I flicked off his shoulder the second time we met; I flicked it into the same oblivion that nail clippings and boogers and tiny sweater fluffs find themselves lost in. And actually I wouldn't want to suck the glaze off his eyes. I should leave it. Because it might be the glaze over his eyes that makes him think I'm so wonderful.

And the sun started to move higher in the sky. It would be shining on The Terrible Thing from that high window above the towel hooks. It might look like a completely different Terrible Thing in that light. Perhaps it might not even look that terrible. Maybe when Julia found The Terrible Thing it would be all emblazoned by that light and she'd be able to come back and say, "You know what? It's not that terrible after all."

Phyllis and her Lawn

The years ploughed by for Phyllis like a cartoon brawl rolling down a hill, picking up speed and random objects, animals, and people as it descended. Her body, the nucleic force of the furious scribble, was absolutely out of control: slipping and falling and flaking off, gaining much, losing little. Every time she attempted to yank back the reins, hoist up some skin, peel back some layers, retaliate against those villainous years, she was royally reprimanded. Time had her by the throat, and the more she squirmed the tighter it gripped.

Yet it had once been effortless.

And it was that effortlessness that she was trying to replicate. But an attempt at effortlessness is a paradox at the very least. And certainly a futile war for Phyllis. Which she fought rigorously at night and in the morning, reserving the day for absolute stillness in the hope that time would just stop noticing her all together.

Each morning, once she'd prepared a cup of coffee, she would sidle herself in front of the bathroom mirror to begin the process of finding her real, day face beneath the old face that she wore to bed. She would pull back the skin around her temples and jawbone until someone else was looking back at her. Then she would tape everything in place carefully, hoisting and tugging here and there to make sure that the tape could withstand all of the sitting and sipping.

In the next step, she scooped two handfuls of brilliantly white cream from an industrial-sized jar and rubbed and rubbed and rubbed it into her face and neck until it was all gone. This cream caused her to look all slimy and tight and sore like duck meat; a wet, wincing eye betrayed its sting.

Then a second cream, a thin layer this time, on top of the other stuff.

And the second cream caused her face to foam white, very suddenly and furiously, bubbles exploding from one another, dripping in hunks from her face to the sink. After a few seconds Phyllis picked up a cloth from a basket on the counter and gave her face a clean swipe from top to bottom, revealing skin as white as porcelain beneath, a mask that seemed to have emerged from that once raw, angry canvas. A scar. Smooth and happy as a firm, white grape.

An army of pots and tubes and jars came down from her cupboard, each with its own instrument. It was time to apply paint to her new mask and arrange her hair just so to hide the tape and clips that she'd used to pull back her bedtime face.

The last step was the examination. Her face so close to the mirror that she left a picture of her breath behind, she scrutinized every angle under the bare bulbs over the mirror, peering into each of her wrinkles and pores, making sure that there was nothing more she could do to make them look better.

When she was done she would turn to me and squint carefully, perhaps suspecting my own odd mirror habits. Julia and I, both in the hallway watching; Phyllis's mask eclipsing the bright, bare bulb over the bathroom mirror. She would smile slightly and step around our bent, compacted bodies, leaving us in the cloud of cosmetic smell that billowed from her housecoat. It was time for her to enter the bedroom and hoist herself into an outfit for the day. We never watched this part.

The lawn, though, really was beautiful. And though this beauty wasn't effortless, it looked as though it could be. Possible that under the right conditions, grass like that could grow naturally from the earth, a rare, fluorescent event in nature. Strange like stars, or the aurora borealis: spells cast from a wand over the sky.

So she would sit in her enclosed porch, as still a butterfly in a crate save for one infrequent twitch: the raising of a teacup to her lips. A living, breathing, sipping shrine for her many admirers, who very often found themselves stopped on the sidewalk in front of her lawn, lips hung from gaping mouths on faces sizzling in green light. Some even dared to speak a word of appreciation from time to time. Phyllis would nod and smile, a mystery in the shadows. She adored being the face accepting credit for that lawn.

Some old ladies kept little dogs or disloyal birds, but Phyllis kept a lawn. It invited hands. Brought life into a dead world, brought light to a dark place. Each little blade was easier to love than anything or anyone she'd ever encountered. These little blades were kind and sweet and cared only for her, worked for her, grew up to be strong and healthy all for her. Phyllis liked to watch them, their stillness disrupted rarely by the wind, which moved each blade differently. She wanted to be as still as they, wanted to be drawn into the dirt and reborn a million times, at the same time, like each little blade of smooth grass.

In the evenings Phyllis would finish her last teacup of the night slowly and have one cigarette from the pack that she kept hidden behind a rung supporting her chair. I'm not exactly sure who she was hiding them from, because she smoked them just as openly as she gave disapproving looks to perfect strangers.

At night, each of her feet was encased in a black slipper, intricately embroidered with gold and silver thread. The colors reminded me of the hair that grew from The Mother's head, gray and yellow, colors almost indiscernible from one another unless suddenly caught by light and held for a moment, stiff with the terror of being discovered. It was just about impossible to keep hold of the distinction for long. The silver and gold thread would confuse themselves in your eyes almost immediately and you'd have to blink to be sure of anything at all. Phyllis's thread drew a picture of a family of little birds eating golden berries from a silver branch. I think. It could have been silver berries from a golden branch.

Her whole body moved ever so slightly, as though she were stuffed with something slithering. Her neck seemed tired, struggling with the weight of her small head, her hair wrapped up in a sheer black scarf. Once, she fell asleep. I watched it happen from the living room window, and at first I didn't know what to do. Julia wouldn't want me waking her up. Julia would prefer Phyllis to wake up in the middle of the night, neck stiff and uncomfortable, feeling strange and unrested like you sometimes do when you fall asleep in jeans. She might even wish that Phyllis catch a cold out there, the kind that devastates older ladies and eventually kills them. But I couldn't do that. So I went outside and shook her just enough so she woke up without being startled and I thought for a moment that I saw The Lonely flash across her face, distort her carefully highlighted features. The same Lonely I saw in The Mother and the same Lonely that would overcome me if I didn't have Julia.

"Sit with me a minute, Easter."

So I did. She finished the contents of her teacup and I followed the outline of the houses across the street with my eyes, carefully separating black house from dark blue sky. They seemed as unreal as a pop-up book.

Lipstick

Julia and I had a lot of conversations with her hanging upside down off the couch in The House, a vine-like vein throbbing in her forehead, her eyes growing redder, all of the blood rushing to her head as though poured slow from a ketchup bottle. She told me about babies like this, where they came from and the terrible ordeal of childbirth.

"You see my face, Easter? How it looks all veiny and strangled? That's what fresh babies look like. You should see it. Horrific. Your vagina rips in two and this purpled, wrinkled creature comes flying out. And you're stuck with it."

"That's horrible." All of the blood scurried from my face. Julia liked to scare me.

"I know."

"Why does anyone do such an awful thing?"

"Because they've got to do it. Everyone's got to."

"Well, I don't want to have a baby!"

"You've got to get one somehow, Easter! Otherwise you'll be a freak with no one to take care of you when you're old and people will look at you and feel bad for you. You don't want to be pitied."

"Why not?"

"I don't really know, but I know that you don't want it. No one ever wants anyone else's pity. In movies anyway."

"Well, I wouldn't mind being pitied."

"That's because you don't know anything yet, Easter. You're still just a kid. You've got to either be a pod or get a baby some other kind of way, otherwise you're a social reject."

"How are you going to get one?"

"I'll just acquire one somehow. In the comical way that hard-working career women accidentally acquire them in movies. That way it won't be my fault. I'll have really tried to have a career, but by some hilarious turn of events I get stuck with a baby and eventually fall in love with it, and change my name to Mommy and get married to a husband who loves the baby."

"Well, I want that too."

"You can't. I'm already doing it."

"I can do it too."

"Fine, Easter, do whatever you want."

Julia pulled her head up and sat backward on the couch, letting her brain readjust to right-side-up reality. She stood up and staggered a bit to the bathroom. I lay on my stomach on the carpet, still staring at the spot on the couch where Julia's face had been. If I closed my eyes the shape of her head remained, seared onto my eyelids, skin glowing.

When I opened my eyes her face was right-side-up in front of me and she was holding a gold tube of lipstick in front of my face. She had fetched The Mother's bag of lipsticks from the bathroom: an ancient, filthy, black-and-white-checkered bag that contained every lipstick The Mother had ever purchased in her entire life. Literally. And she was very proud of that accomplishment. The Mother was as proud of her mangy bag of lipsticks as some people are of their stamp collections or rare comic books. Evidence, to herself and others, of her immovable motivation, her ability to commit to and complete tasks, her passion about things outside of her family. Because apparently that's what a giant bag of lipsticks says about a person.

Julia plucked a gooey Pink Rose Petal to apply to her lips and I picked up an orangey red called Autumn Rust. Lipstick was an easy answer to boredom. It was the most exciting thing you could do in the shortest amount of time because for a second, you got to convince yourself that you were the kind of gal who wears lipstick every day. You got to pout to yourself, and trick yourself that you were glamorous. Then in a second it was over, time to wipe it off and start again.

Sometimes when I was in the bath or on the toilet and The Mother was folding laundry in our room we would read the colors out to her and she would reply with the corresponding number code or vice versa. It was actually quite fun.

"4207," I would squeal.

"Sugar Plum Fairy. Sparkly purple. I wore it in 1989 to a friend's birthday party. We went to a club called Wavelength. Isn't that an awful name? Sounds like a Barbie Nightclub. Next!"

"6399," I hollered.

"Fire Engine Red."

"Yeah, that's right! You're amazing."

"That's my sixth tube of that stuff, thanks to you."

We had destroyed many a tube of that particular color over the years, on account of a game that Julia made up.

It went like this:

She would drag the Fire Engine Red across her wrists and mock a very dramatic suicide. Then, when I would pretend to investigate the scene, she would leap up and slit my throat with it, at which point I would attempt to perform an even more realistic death than she had because in the game, this one was real. We were practicing this scenario, among others, with some frequency for a while, seeing how long we could lie still, how discreetly we could move our chests as we breathed. A few times I walked in on Julia lying in front of the tall bathroom mirror, watching herself perform death so she could get better and better at it.

The problem is, you can't fake dead hands. That invisible something that fills dead or sleeping hands, making them appear strange and inanimate, is impossible to imitate. The Mother couldn't do it in the bathtub on Sunday nights, though she tried so hard to imitate it, and we couldn't do it in our game.

After a while The Mother got wise to this misuse of her precious lipsticks, which, incidentally, was wearing them out and making them flat so she couldn't use them properly. She told me that we had to stop or she'd take them away and hide them in a closet somewhere far beyond our reach. But it was fun while it lasted.

One afternoon, before we were found out, I walked in on Julia lying still on the floor in front of the mirror, covered in fatal slashes of Fire Engine Red. I sat down on the edge of the tub and looked down at her face. With her eyes still closed she said:

"Sometimes I feel like I'm disappearing."

She looked particularly pale and her clothes hung over her prone body like a sheet over a corpse at a crime scene. Her lips had taken on the whitish quality of someone who'd been trapped in a meat locker for a couple of hours, and beneath her eyes hung hammocks of bluish-gray skin. I'll never forget the way that her face looked on this day, which is probably why it's this face of hers that keeps flashing in my head as I lie under this big, stupid rock.

I didn't really know how to respond to her statement, so I said,

"You know, you really look like a corpse right now. How did you do that?"

"I've been practicing."

I furrowed my brow at her, smiling. Our inside joke.

"Your face, though, it's all blue.

"I'm dead, Easter. I drowned this afternoon. Had a seizure throwing up and fell-face first into the toilet."

"Why were you throwing up?"

"Because I'm feeling sad, Easter, that's why."

"Why?"

"Because one day you'll lose me and then you won't be special anymore. You'll be just like everyone else."

I'm You

Shortness of breath. That's one of the first signs of kidney failure. And I'm pretty sure I had it. Kidney failure that is. And shortness of breath for that matter. My cigar-butt stumps were almost black, and as shiny and smooth and full and firm as concord grapes, and the color was reaching up into my shorts.

In a weird way I kind of felt like Snow White or Cinderella or one of those other princesses who are surrounded by woodland creatures, so good and sweet and special that even cute little animals are drawn to me and show me, only me, how helpful and aware they are. If only Lev could walk up right when a little blue bird is fluttering down upon one of my elegantly outstretched fingers.

But actually I didn't want him to find me. And I didn't want anyone else to find me either. I was fine with this kind of death, bleeding slowly. I wanted it for myself. I liked the smell of The Woods and sounds of the leaves and the way more and more squirrels seemed to be growing comfortable with me. Plus I had nowhere else to go—I couldn't face Mrs. Bellows after last night, or any of the girls who'd been in the Craft Room. And The Terrible Thing was in The Tooth House. So I might as well just live as a ghost in The Woods. Be as unreal as Julia. Two strange girls living in the strange, unreal world, so in it we'd actually be normal. Normal and together, an impossible combination for us in the regular, real world.

I ground my shoulders deeper into the forest floor, moving them in wide circles to work my way in. I dipped my hands in the pools of blood at my sides and rubbed them on my face. That way I would look far worse off than I already was and maybe some stranger walking by wouldn't rush or anything to try and save me.

And then the wind exhaled through The Woods and cooled the blood on my cheeks, brushing the hair off my forehead and dragging knuckles softly across my face, running a cool finger beneath the ring of my shirt collar the way The Mother would sometimes do on hot days after she'd been rummaging through the freezer. It always put a smile on my face, involuntary, as though she were turning a dial around the base of my neck that made my grin grow wider and wider. I always yelped at her to stop. "Cut it out!" I'd whine, but she'd caught my smile and would do it again.

The wind made me wonder why I'd rubbed this blood all over my face. Why I didn't want anyone to find me. It reminded me that I wasn't the only person on earth. Because that can happen in a stripe of woods. I could easily forget that I'm just one girl, like many other girls. And most other girls lying in The Woods, bleeding, crushed beneath a rock, would be scared and worried and screaming for help. Maybe even praying. They certainly wouldn't feel relieved, or take comfort in the idea of not existing anymore. But then again, they'd probably never seen anything like The Terrible Thing, so it didn't seem fair to compare.

Though I really must remember to remember: I am one of many *I*s. In fact, to everyone else in the world, I'm *you*. And the wind helped me to remember that, like a loud noise or a bucket of water splashed into my face, pulling me from a dream. Which I suppose I appreciated in some ways, but in other ways I very much didn't. I'm you, I'm you, I'm you. I'm I, I'm I, I'm I. I'm two people at once, always, and so are you.

And suddenly fast footsteps cut through brittle leaves, louder and louder until they stopped somewhere above my head. A shadow on the forest floor.

I looked up and saw Julia. Had she seen The Terrible Thing? A ball of something vile formed in my throat and my heart gathered steam, pumping loud enough to keep the death-eating bugs away. I couldn't tell from her face.

"Julia…" I began, but couldn't continue. I needed to know if she'd seen it before I could speak.

"Easter. The door's locked. I need your keys."

I exhaled loudly and the tears that had nestled in the corners of my eyes, perched and ready to fall, sucked themselves back in from where they came. No need to cry yet. She hadn't seen it. The Terrible Thing still might never have happened because *only I* saw it. And *I* could never really be sure of anything I saw. Until Julia confirmed it anyway. Because she's the only person I'd ever really trusted; the only person I could really believe.

"I'm sorry I left you down here, Julia."

She made her way down the side of the cliff, ignoring me, complaining about the inconvenience of having to come back for the keys.

"I said I'm sorry I left you here," I repeated.
"I know," she said.
"When this is all over I'll come and stay with you. We can live here together."
"We'll see about that."

I could hear her huffing and puffing as she moved from her legs to her bum where the side of the cliff got steep. Pebbles trickled down with her, cracking against the rocks at the bottom.

"Why'd you rub blood all over your face?" she asked, puzzled and out of breath.

I'd forgotten about that.

"I don't know. Nothing else to do."

She nodded. "Why don't you count something?"

"Like what?"

"I don't know, leaves. Count the leaves. I've already counted them a few times. Let's see if we get the same number."

What a good idea. How could I have ever left her here? How could I have ever lived without her? What was I thinking? I felt more like my real self now than I had in weeks. Even though I was technically only half of myself.

She crunched over to me, reached into my pocket, and pulled out the bloody keys.

"You're lucky these didn't get crushed," she said.

And made her way back up the side of the cliff and toward The House.

The First Bridle

After all the tunnel work was done, the real search could begin. The first tunnel led us through a million pictures of Phyllis the Fucking Bitch. One picture in a gradient of grays, Phyllis the focus in a white bathroom, half sitting on the sink; she couldn't have been more than twenty, her blonde hair cut in a short bob, her body wrapped in a dark towel, her face turned away from us but visible in a bathroom mirror. She stares at herself with a finger under her chin, pushing it up, stretching her twisted neck uncomfortably. Her eyes are all admiring, her lips parted slightly, her face unnaturally relaxed considering the awkward angle of the rest of her body. It scared me to see her looking so young, to see how much she'd changed, but Julia kept looking. I insisted that we move on, so we did.

Then Julia said my name. I looked up at her standing next to Elizabeth's equine inhaler. I think. A clear, plastic muzzle with a little opening for fastening an asthma puffer, and a leather strap so it stays on the horse's head. An ornate, cursive *E* embossed into the thickest part of the strap, likely standing for Elizabeth.

"One down."

Over the course of that day we uncovered Elizabeth's gas mask, her respiratory measurement mask and her armor. Phyllis seemed satisfied with our progress. Over dinner she told us so.

"You're actually not doing a bad job."
"Thanks."
"Think you can find the rest of them by Thursday?"
"I think so. We've got a whole system of tunnels worked out so that we can hit every square inch of that cube."
"Cube?"
"The basement."
"Right. How do you like your jam casserole?"
"It's delicious."
"Good."

Phyllis drank the last gulp from her teacup, washed it, and headed upstairs to get ready for bed. Julia and I remained at the table.

"Easter? I've changed my mind. I want to do something nice for Phyllis."
"Yeah right."

"No really. Maybe she's not all bad. We should do something good for her."

"Why have you changed your mind?"

"The granola bars and the chocolate milk. She doesn't want us to die down there. Maybe she just wants us to know more about her."

"And for us to get those horse masks so that she doesn't have to."

"Well, yeah, but maybe, also, she just doesn't know how to talk to us because she's so weird."

"Well, what do you want to do for her?"

"I have a secret plan. It's going to be a lot of fun."

"Couldn't we just tell her that we want to be friends?"

"Oh yeah, she'd like that way more. What's us telling her we wanna be friends going to show her? That we don't care enough to actually *do* something special, that's what."

"Okay, what's The Plan?"

The Plan

Julia and I dressed in black clothes: black tights with black sweaters; black socks and our dirtiest sneakers. We'd spent the whole day altering the antique horse bridles that we'd found so that they'd fit and put them on to disguise our faces. I wore the equine inhaler and Julia wore the equine respiratory mask. They were tight and the bit was fun to chew on. With our backpacks strapped firmly to our shoulders, we each took tiny tiptoed steps out the sliding door, which we left open behind us to make for a faster escape once we were finished with The Plan.

We moved quickly over Phyllis's lawn like it was a hot rock and our feet were bare: picking them up fast, finding cool relief within the shadow of the sphincter-mouthed neighbor's house. Pulling off our knapsacks and crouching against the wall; his bricks were night-cold against our warm backs. It was time to unload the goods. We reached in and removed four large bottles of bleach we'd found in

91

the basement that we'd wrapped in clothes to prevent them from clocking against one another, a most certain consequence of Julia and me attempting to be nimble.

Each holding a bottle of bleach, we took slow, careful steps to the middle of the neighbor's lawn. We looked at one another once, each smiling drool around our antique bridles.

With two gloved fingers, Julia twirled the tip of an invisible moustache, and before another moment had time to pass, the dance of the dick drawing was underway. Beethoven's Third Symphony started blaring in my head. Not because I was really into classical music or anything, it's just the only one I knew really well, and in that moment Julia and I reminded me of two figure skaters sailing across the rink. The sound of our feet shuffling and our heavy breath sputtering wet through the bridles completely drowned by the music.

We skated over the grass, bottles pouring, bleach swimming over the lawn like a living wave. It glowed in the darkness like some demonic crack in the earth, lighting us from the bottom the way that bright white ice might. We took a moment to look at what we had created. Long, straight shaft, a big pair of hairy balls. A perfect dick to start the show.

We each still had three bottles of bleach left and I was only in the second movement of the symphony, which continued to fill our ears as thick as liquid. So we decided to move on to the next lawn. The first dick had brought a shallow flood of illumination to the night. The next dick would make it even brighter. We would have to move faster than I'd first thought.

As we leapt to the next lawn I watched Julia in mid-air, saw her red hair whip in the wind, lashing her long white neck and then settling down immediately like a mink stole over her shoulders when we landed. Our bridles must have clanked loudly as we hit the ground because Julia struck out her lips with one gloved finger. I wondered if she could hear the music too. I'm sure she could because she moved to it as perfectly as I did. Two parts, swirling and twirling and gliding and bleaching together completely. I wanted this night forever.

Another beautiful performance by Easter and Julia. With Easter starting from the bottom and Julia from the top, the two girls meet in the middle of the dick and spin in unison, spraying a healthy smattering of speckled hair onto the perfectly round balls. These girls are masters of the bleach bottle.

For the next lawn, they move together, Julia behind with her hand on Easter's waist. They move backward, shaping the head of the dick, both of their hands on one bottle. Now they leap onto either side with a double axle to begin on the balls. And yes, yes! They appear to be perfectly symmetrical!

Our last lawn. The third movement. We were tired, but there was just one more bottle of bleach and one more lawn to do so that the lawns on both sides of Phyllis's had big, handsome dicks on them.

The last one we poured slowly, carefully. We didn't want to

slip up on the very last dick of the night. And we didn't. Each of the hairs on this final pair of nuts we flourished with glorious swirls as we glided in circles around each other. Julia took hold of the reins on my horse bridle and I got a fist around hers; then we leaned back, pulling down on each other's faces, forming the shape of those last balls as we spun along the same circle. Over and over and over again so everything felt charged and electric and magic in dawn's strange light.

My heart beat fast. Fast as the early morning squirrels as they wrenched flowers out of the dirt by their roots and threw them at our dewy, grass-stained sneakers. A few held up little bits of cardboard with tens drawn on them. A perfect score. Once we were done we took a second to bow to them, and we gathered a few of the flowers in our arms to show our appreciation.

As quickly and quietly as we had emerged from Phyllis's tickled house, we returned, having closed the sliding door only once through the whole operation, Phyllis never even fluttering an eyelash as she slept. I worried for a moment that we might have let the wind out, but Julia assured me that it was still around, making an obstacle course of the candelabra in Phyllis's dining room.

Both of us collapsed into bed, removing only our shoes and our bridles before we fell and smiled ourselves to sleep, the final movement of Beethoven's third like water in a hot pan on my brain.

Our First

The next morning I awoke to the sounds of Phyllis laughing. A loud, rich laugh that excited the trapped wind. Pictures rattled, curtains moved. Without opening my eyes, I reached over to feel if Julia was still there. She wasn't. Phyllis's laughter was interrupted by a voice. I stepped out of bed and took off my black clothes. Julia must have already stuffed hers somewhere inconspicuous. Phyllis was responding to the voice and both of them were getting louder. I found a warm and rumpled nightie beneath the radiator and pulled it over my head, shushed my feet in a pair of slippers and snuck quietly down the hall to listen to the commotion. I kneeled at the top of the stairs. The voices were coming from the porch and the front door was open. The other voice was Norman from next door.

"I can't believe you're laughing at this," quivered the voice of Norman.

He was in shock, I think.

"But Norman, it's quite funny. Can't you see how it's funny?"

"For you, maybe. Yours is the only lawn unscathed!"

"Thank goodness for that."

I peeked through the spindles of the banister and could see half of the back of Phyllis. She wore a tan, one-piece linen suit with a big white belt. It made her look like she was going on a safari. In front of Phyllis I could see half of the front of Norman. I could tell even from a section of his face that he was furious.

"Why, Phyllis? Why would your lawn be the only one without a—that hasn't been defaced."

"I don't know. Maybe someone around here has a little crush on me."

"Phyllis, this is vandalism, do you realize that? Vandalism is a crime."

My throat caught a ball of air.

"Imagine me, a grandmother for goodness' sake, being charged with vandalism."

"I don't know how you can make jokes right now. When Dorothy and Al and the others see their lawns, it won't be so easy to deny everything."

"Norman, I haven't done anything."

"Tell it to the judge, Phyllis!"

"All right, Norman! Come by later if you want to borrow some fertilizer. It looks like you'll need it."

I heard Norman's door slam. Phyllis turned around and walked inside. She looked right at me—could she see some part of me hanging out past the wall? Oh no. I moved back very slowly. I think she saw me. She definitely saw me. I braved the hungry carpet on my hands and knees, crawling back to our room, and tried to listen through the floor for any clue as to how Phyllis was feeling. I felt the beat of her heels against the kitchen floor as she paced. I don't know what she was thinking down there, but her feet sounded angry. I waited until the breakfast invitation was officially fifteen minutes past due to realize that she probably didn't want to see me at all today.

I decided it was best to hide until she went outside again, and then sneak down into the basement to spend the rest of the day.

After some rustling in the kitchen, I finally heard the front screen door close and the sound of Phyllis's teacup settling in its saucer on the table next to her porch chair. I listened to her pick it up, drink from it presumably, then put it back down on the table again. This happened a few times, enough for me to feel as though she were safely settled out there for a while. I snuck down the stairs, careful to avoid the creaks. Just as I was about to open the basement door, I heard the screen peel from the doorframe and Phyllis's foot hit the floor. I froze, neck stiff, shoulders pulled up to my ears.

"Good morning, Easter," she said, already leaned over, pulling on her slippers, a steadying hand on the banister.

"Hi." My top teeth settled into my bottom lip as I waited for her next words.

"Easter, look at me for a minute."

So I turned and looked at her, and the faintest smile momentarily cracked her lacquered face, gone so fast I wasn't sure if it was ever really there.

"You know I'm going to have to tell your mother about this. She'll ask me about the lawns as soon as she comes in. And I won't lie to her for you, if that's what you were expecting. She should know, because I think you're strange, and what you did was a strange thing to do."

"I didn't do it."

Her face might have cracked again. My heart pounded, powered by the lie, filling my ears with blood, the sound of cupped hands.

"Easter, of course you did."

"No, I didn't do it. I mean, I have no idea what you're talking about. Do what?"

Goddammit, I should have opened with "I have no idea what you're talking about." Julia would have thought of that— where was she? Phyllis nodded, walked past me, and proceeded with whatever it was she'd planned to do in the kitchen.

I turned around and entered the basement, closing the door behind me. I found Julia already in The Café picking at a plate of leftover jam casserole that she'd somehow managed to acquire.

"Where the hell were you this morning?"

"What?"

"We're in so much trouble, Julia, I don't even know what to do. We committed a crime out there. Those dicks are a crime!"

"Oh they are not. And they can't prove anything either. I got rid of the empty bottles this morning. You're welcome."

"What did you do with them?"

"I can't tell you. No one else should know but me."

"All right, fine. But we've really got to find the rest of Phyllis's bridles today so that she doesn't hate us forever. We got her in a lot of trouble with Norman, you know. And probably the rest of the neighbors."

"But she laughed. She liked it. It made her happy."

"Maybe at first, but not now. Now she can't possibly be happy with us—hey, where'd you get the casserole? I'm starving."

"Phyllis left it for us at the door."

For the rest of our stay, we worked as quietly as we could, careful to avoid Phyllis on the main floor at all costs, listening to the floorboards for the stress of her weight. And I uncovered my secret anatomy book. A large anatomy book with the cross-section of a tooth all yellow and pulpy on the inside. And could think only of our house, hard and smooth and normal on the outside but filled with unexpected squishiness on the inside. Unexpected interior soreness all red and ready to rot if exposed. Our house was a tooth, and I could see it so clearly in these waxy pages spread open in front of me. And suddenly the spine of the book felt like a cold snake between my thighs. So I closed it up promptly and shoved it deep into The Cube.

That same day we found a large metal ring covered in mink pelts, the ring feeding through the holes where their eyes used to be. They smelled cold, dust and leather and something else. Julia pulled the ring up around her leg like a garter belt, then stood up and turned from side to side to make the pelts spin and slap against her.

Then she held her leg out in front of my face.

"Pull it off," she said.

So I did.

Then I put it on my own leg and Julia pulled it off. She dragged her fingers along my legs and made me jump, startled by the feeling. Her fingers were colder than usual.

By the time Thursday rolled around the entire cube was colonized, each room decorated to our liking, piles of stuff to look through. We even had a mystery on our hands that took the form of a shoebox full of wallets containing drivers' licenses from all over the country, expiry dates going back to the early 1980s.

We were perusing the last receipts from each wallet, trying to find a clue as to why they were here in the basement. It seemed as though the last things these men purchased were flowers and boxes of chocolate, typical gifts of endearment for people that you don't know very well.

Julia was beginning to formulate a theory most sinister when we heard Phyllis calling to us from outside The Cube. She would stick her head into the first tunnel and speak so that by the time her voice reached us it had accumulated a ghostly quality, heard perfectly and not at all. The Mother and Father were here to pick us up and it was time to say goodbye. We decided to leave the wallets, just in case they might incriminate us for some crime in the future. All the bridles had been found but one: the regular bridle still remained lost in The Cube. One final bridle that I would find years and years later, wedged between two rocks in The Woods.

Julia began to gather our jammed and crumby toast plates and with her back turned I reached into the spot where I'd shoved the anatomy book and pulled it out and slid it secretly into my red backpack, concealing the corners with rolled-up socks. I did this all very quickly, so quickly that Julia didn't even notice.

I started making my way through the first tunnel off The Café, wanting to leave Julia before she could tell I had a secret. But I must have dislodged something when I removed the book, some very important structural item, because suddenly The Café began to shake and rumble like a space pod about to launch. Julia, her hands full of plates, whipped around and looked at me, terrified, before The Café collapsed and crushed her completely.

Trickles of blood reached out of the dusty pile of decimated café as though trying to escape.

And I felt terrible. Not only that I'd killed my sister and only friend, but that I'd have to face The Mother and her lecture about the dick drawings all alone. On elbows and knees, I worried my way out through the main tunnel for the very last time and vowed that if I ever saw Julia again, I'd never ever tell her about the anatomy book that helped kill her.

Squirrel

There was one good thing about being stuck beneath this rock: it shaded me very nicely. All of the dirt around my face and hands was cool and sandy and I kept rubbing my cheeks against it, like it could feel me back. I love cold earth in the summertime, morning earth, nice and raw before it begins to bake. I was breathing deeply and letting the little blades of grass that were reaching toward me from below the world tickle and poke at my nose and sleepy eyelids. I didn't really want to close my eyes all the way if I didn't have to in these woods. I didn't want anything around here to think that I was dead yet. But the sun was moving over me and it felt so nice to rest my eyes.

The back of my eyelids looked red, sunlight through flesh. Almost the color of my bandana. Warm and folded flat in my back pocket. I'd been wearing it all the time these days. Or at least carrying it with me, so that if it got windy I could put it on my head to keep my hair from getting all twisted up, or if I'd just eaten a gyro and was feeling really gross I could wear it over my face like a cowboy. It's actually not really red—more of a maroon color. Like a bad bruise, so purple that it's red. Julia hated it and would have teased me for wearing it again. Lev said he thought it was nice.

With my eyes closed, I thought about the day I'd found it. Spotted it between two paint cans at the place where The Father got his clarinet cleaned. While he was busy talking to the man behind the counter, I stood with my back to the cans, right close up so I could touch a little purpled end of the haggard thing. It was soft and thin and cool. I pulled it out gently and stuffed it up the sleeve of my sweatshirt. It tickled the inside of my forearm and stopped my heart from beating so fast.

The man who I was stealing from had a long, thin neck, curved lumbarlike to support his large cranium. He had black hair that stood up straight, and big round eyes that seemed just barely pressed into his head. Bulging. Raindrops held still upon a waxy leaf. I thought about how easy it would be to remove them, flick them off his face like marbles. As he spoke he manipulated a long brush in his hands, dragging his fingers along its short bristles, moving it in and out of a helpless clarinet that I'd just watched him de-skirt and decapitate.

I could never hear his voice. When he opened his mouth all I heard was an erratic clarinet. I hadn't come here very often and after I stole the bandana I never went back again.

As we left through the dinging front door, I couldn't stop smiling. It felt like I had some small creature in my sleeve. A cute little alien that I could teach hilarious and adorable phrases to, like in the movies. And it wouldn't judge me for whatever issue I had—like divorced parents or a disability or something. It would be my best friend.

As we made our way to the car, I noticed that The Father didn't reach for me. I forget when he stopped holding my hand through parking lots. I remember wondering if he still held Julia's, knowing very well that she didn't have a hand for him to hold anyway.

A wheezy squeak blew away my memory, very quiet like a broken toy, somewhere behind my head, deeper in The Woods. I opened my eyes a bit, let them refocus just to be sure I was still alone. But I wasn't alone. A little squirrel was staring at me. Right up close. Well, as close as I'd ever been to a wild rodent. He was gray, with a tail that looked like a wad of cotton candy and a twitchy little nose that couldn't stay still. His eyes were black and tiny and his hands were filled with a fast-food cheeseburger that had a big human bite taken out of it. Someone must have thrown it out of their car.

Carrying the great big cheeseburger was clearly an enormous task for this little squirrel. I could see that he was paranoid that I was going to try and steal it from him. I wished there were some way for me to tell him that I would never, ever hurt him. "Eat it, buddy," I rasped at the squirrel. "Eat it! And then you won't have to carry it around anymore." I twisted a bit around the middle so I could see him better and my insides groaned like an old hinge. It was as though my whole body was turning into the same tough wood that my cigar-nub thighs already were. My heart thundered from the effort.

He carried the burger closer to me, arms low, bitty hands stressed to their absolute capacity, his feet shuffling close to the ground under the weight of the once-smooth bun, now freckled with indentations from his clumsy, piercing fingers. The burger's guts were all the brown and white of meat and onion skins, harried by twigs and grass. A smear of ketchup dried into the fur beneath the squirrel's chin. He took a few tentative steps closer, his tapered snout up in the air, suspicious eyes all over and inspecting me. Once he'd decided I wasn't a threat he promptly flopped the burger down and started to feast, tearing off chunks with his quick little claws and then munching them at a million frenzied bites per second.

It was adorable.

Julia would have loved this so much if she were here. If she were lying next to me the way I loved her to, the soft spot behind her ears soaked in the cool shadow of her lobe. And I'd just left her here with no one to talk to or play with but the squirrels. I deserved this. Being stuck under this rock. I loved Julia and I'd treated her horribly. She was the first person I wanted to see when I found The Terrible Thing, she was the only person I'd be able to talk to, the only person who could understand how terrible The Terrible Thing was. How guilty The Terrible Thing made me feel. The Terrible Thing. Our lipstick game made real. I wanted to tell her that it felt nothing like the game, that it looked nothing like the game; all the details that made it different, made us wrong for even pretending. But she wasn't here, so I made The Terrible Thing go away again.

The Mother loved little critters doing human things too. She once cut out a picture from the paper of a frog on a toy motorcycle and kept it tucked into the mirror on her vanity for years and years. She would have been rubbing her hands together and kicking her feet up and oohing and ahhing over and over again until you couldn't help but laugh.

Suddenly the squirrel shot up straight as an arrow, like someone had flicked a switch in his spine. His ears seemed to rotate in his head, moving around then fixing themselves at impossible angles. He could hear something. But what? I couldn't hear anything but the symphony of woodsy sounds I'd been hearing all morning. I tried to pry into the symphony, pick something unique from the rustling and the tweeting and the crackling. A thread I could follow to a perfectly logical source. But seeing as I had no idea what I was listening for, it was very difficult.

The squirrel's bitsy eyes darted back and forth feverishly. Body so still I could almost see his chest hammering. He seemed nervous. Which made me very nervous. Something was inching toward us and only this little guy could hear it coming, and even if he could warn me somehow there was nowhere I could go.

I looked around as much as I could, beads of sweat growing from my pores like tubers. I couldn't see anything. I closed my eyes tight and tried to listen harder; more shuffling, breathing, the sound of a pair of nervous feet suddenly stopped in their tracks, but I heard nothing and soon grew too scared to keep my eyes closed any longer.

When I looked back, the little squirrel was gone. He'd abandoned me because he was scared and he could. He'd left the remains of his burger splayed out over a placemat of green and yellow leaves. Green and yellow, incidentally the worst flavor of gummy snake ever. And the colors of the June Room. But we won't be sent there for a very long time still. Not until after I ruin us at The Lake House.

Julia Returns After Being Crushed by The Cube

The Parents were bewildered and disappointed and confused. The Mother cried, The Father shook his head, and I still had Julia to face, who'd be furious about my accidentally killing her. I sat alone in my room, "grounded," which meant nothing to a girl without friends.

I'm terrible at making friends. The worst actually. No one likes me and I don't blame them. I wouldn't like the me that gets introduced to people. I twitch my nose in social situations; suddenly it begins to feel very uncomfortable just sitting there in the middle of my face and I must twitch it. I avoid eye contact. I laugh at things that are sad, like when the fat girl told me that her cat died and all I could do was laugh in her face. Julia doesn't help, either. She's the one who started me laughing at the fat girl. When I asked the fat girl why she was crying and she replied, "my cat died," Julia popped up behind her and said, "And don't forget, you're fat too." It was hilarious.

But the lying; the lying is the most embarrassing. Even as I'm doing it, I know it's not going to end well. My hackles swell as I speak, in readiness for the certain onslaught of naysayers. I'm the reason that partners have to be assigned in school instead of chosen, or why teachers have to pick the teams in gym class instead of letting kids separate on their own. Once you've spit something out, you can't eat it back up again. People don't forget.

I picture myself sitting in front of a plate of all of the lies I've told over the years: wet, masticated, homogenous piles like chewed-up mouthfuls of Thanksgiving dinner: mashed potatoes, corn, turkey, gravy. Only instead they're piles of my steaming lies: "I'm going to Paris this summer," "My mom wrote that song actually," "I used to be a professional figure skater but my parents made me quit to be a normal kid," "I have four chinchillas." I have to eat them all back up again, plate after plate, chunky and oily and burning and slopping on my shirt in a big greasy stain. It's revolting. I usually have to close my eyes and shake my head before that thought fully dissolves. Prickling nausea remains.

I've had many lies exposed over the years, quite publicly. In other words I'm well known as the weird liar, in addition to being incredibly awkward. So, really, the best I can hope for is that people just leave me alone. Bizarre lies linger in school hallways like an odor, as worried into the air as the smell of pencil shavings. But honestly, I don't really want to get to know most people anyway. Most people are boring assholes. Secretly I am better than everyone.

To me, being grounded means that I just end up sleeping a lot. And after one of my many naps I woke up to Julia scowling at me.

"Julia!" I shrieked, and grabbed her fast as though she might disappear again.

"You killed me!"

"I didn't mean to, Julia, it was an accident."

"It was an accident."

"Well, of course it was!"

"Yeah, well, accident or no, you still killed me. Now you're a murderer."

"Oh I am not."

"You are. You killed someone."

"Hardly."

"What's that supposed to mean?"

"Nothing."

"No really, Easter, what do you mean by that? That you hardly killed me? Or I'm hardly someone?"

"Julia, please. I'm sorry, okay?"

And I inched closer to her, so she got off the bed and looked out the window.

"Have you seen this?" she asked, gesturing at something outside.

"What?" I got up and looked.

Amelia from next door was in the car with her boyfriend.

Amelia's life was pretty much perfect except for her being boring and stupid and having a face like a primordial dwarf. She had her own bathroom and a pink canopy bed with ruffles along the bottom. It was like one of those beds you see in department store magazines that you can set up whole daydreams around, in which even just circling items longingly in pen is somehow satisfying. When I sat down on it I felt like a princess. Or at least a princess's creepy acquaintance. I'd only seen it once, when the neighbors invited us over to dinner. Really they just wanted to ask The Parents to collect their mail and water their garden while they were on vacation.

Since they'd started dating a year ago, Julia and I had been watching the progression of Amelia and her boyfriend's physical relationship. In horror. Through the backseat windows of his Ford Mercury Sable.

He was a greasy troll of a senior whose early adolescent acne had left him with hoof marks in his cheeks.

"Amelia's really got the worst face I've ever seen," Julia finally said.

"Her body's okay, though. That's why she's always got a boyfriend."

"Whenever I can just see her leg or a bit of her hair or shoulder in the car window, she seems much prettier."

"Yeah. If only she could somehow be just one great eye. Or a bit of long-haired scalp over a shoulder. Instead of her whole gross self," I replied.

"No wonder serial killers liked to chop up women,"

Julia said. "They seem so much better when they're just bits and pieces."

"I'd rather be one perfect leg than my whole self."

And Julia laughed.

"I'm really sorry I killed you, Julia."
"I know."
"Did it hurt?"
"No."
"Good."

We stared for a while in silence as perfect bits and pieces of Amelia appeared and disappeared from the window.

"Maybe we should do Amelia the favor of cutting her up," Julia suddenly said, her eyes never leaving the car.

I laughed but she didn't. She just kept looking. And I got the feeling I sometimes get. When Julia got ideas that I couldn't say no to. Like the bleached lawns at Phyllis's, or when we were small, hiding from The Mother so long that she cried.

"Maybe it would make Amelia's life easier if she could be just one perfect leg," Julia said.

And I realized that she hadn't blinked in a long time. Then she placed a hand on the cold glass. Fog formed between her warm fingers.

I crawled back into the bed, pulled the covers over my head, and shoved the heels of my hands into my eye sockets so hard that I got a headache.

Easter Story

"Stop squiggling your toes."

"I can't help it. Every time you get near them with that marker they go crazy."

"Well you have to try and stop, Easter, it's impossible to trace a squiggling foot."

"All right, I know, you're right."

Easter's eyes narrowed a bit and little creases found their places in her fresh, eleven-year-old skin, her lips stiff as door wedges. This was the face of determination. Julia had a hand wrapped around Easter's left ankle, holding her foot snug to the underside of the dining room table and with a green magic marker in the other hand began to lean forward, a second attempt at producing a permanent record of Easter's foot. Easter could barely stand the excitement. As soon as she felt Julia's breath on the tops of her feet she started squiggling and couldn't stop.

"Goddammit, Easter!"

"Don't swear! Mom'll hear," Easter replied with her feet still pressed against the table.

"No she won't."

"She will too! She's sitting up there with her crossword. I'm looking at her knees right now."

"Easter, you're not even talking. No one can hear anything."

"Okay, right. I promise I won't squiggle again."

"All right."

Julia tightened her grasp on Easter's ankle and let her nails dig too deep into the dip between bone and tendon above her heel. That seemed to stop the squiggling. Worked for horses too. Now two perfectly traced feet looked down at them from the roof of their little world beneath the table.

"Good job, Julia. I love them."

"You're welcome. Okay, now do me."

But Julia's feet always looked strange when Easter traced them onto the table. Nothing like her feet in real life.

Over the years, Easter and Julia had drawn a full mural on the underside of the dining room table: mermaids, blocks of cheese, dogs serving chicken dinners to their masters, orchards of cigarette trees, pipes, squiggles, plates of spaghetti, a rainbow, snails in too-tight ties performing stand-up comedy routines, little girls sweating buckets with big bows in their hair, tracings of growing feet. They drew vines up the sides of the sturdy wooden legs in green magic marker and rammed colored tacks into the support beams, stuck a few scattered glow-in-the-dark stars in the corners. Sometimes they would acquire bits of ribbon in the strange and mysterious way that houses seem to acquire things like that, and they would hang them from the roof of the table like streamers.

For some reason that they could only guess at, it was warmer under the table. Perhaps it was because The Parents shuffled their legs under there, generating heat, or maybe they were directly above the furnace in the basement. Either way, they never needed socks and would rub their feet together in their pajamas, short pants exposing their delicate ankles. They would attempt to intertwine their toes with little success. Neither of the girls had very elegant feet, though later in life Julia would be able to pluck from a bowl and feed herself long snacks like pretzel sticks and smoke a cigarette down to the middle using only her toes.

And they both felt much prettier. They brought mirrors under there and makeup but not nail polish. The Father had said that it made him nauseous to smell it while he ate and they both decided that that was fair enough. They learned to flip their eyelids in the dim light beneath the table. They pulled each other's fingers to the disgust of The Parents and their own wicked delight. The Parents ate smelly food up above and talked about money. Easter and Julia ate licorice and clipped as many clothespins to their faces as they could.

On special occasions The Parents would lay a dark cloth over the table, and Easter and Julia would enter their fort slowly, dramatically. It seemed a more solemn, beautiful place when the *tablecloth quieted everything. Not a place for squealing laughter and violent thumb wars or fights about squiggling toes.*

After dinner on those tablecloth nights, The Parents usually went upstairs and left the girls to play, shutting off every light but the one in the bathroom so they could still spot it in the dark. The girls would turn on flashlights and tell stories, illuminating sections of the mural and their own curvaceous faces, letting the light change the look of everything.

Some nights the darkness of The House would sneak under the cloth and fill their wide-awake bodies; previously busy hands were loaded with the mysterious weight of sleep. Easter knew that hands were always the worst giveaway in a pretend sleep attempt, sleeping hands being impossible to fake. She would later learn that the same was true of pretend deaths when she and Julia started playing the lipstick game, and when she'd watch her mother imitate death on Sunday nights in the bathtub. What was that invisible girth that filled them?

So the sleep would fill them up and keep them warm until The Parents emerged from wherever they'd been and carried the two of them to their room, their hands perhaps threatening to fill with wake as they were carried up the stairs.

Many times one or the other had whacked a head while coming out from or going under that table. Easter had a scar on her forehead to remember the time when she took a brisk, routine dive beneath the table and woke up to Julia's deflated, worried face spilling over her.

"Good, you're not dead," Julia said, and then disappeared into the basement.

Easter sat up. The Mother had heard it from upstairs and came barrelling down the steps with dye in her hair.

"Easter, my god, what did you do?"

That's when Easter felt the trickle down her forehead, a nimble plop on her upper lip. She tasted it. Like pennies. The Mother shrieked and Easter cried, though it didn't really hurt.

She took Easter by the arm, grabbed the keys, and within ten minutes they'd checked in at Emergency and were both crammed into a small hospital bathroom while The Mother washed the dye out of her hair over the sink. Easter stood on the lid of the toilet, her right hand holding a square of gauze to her forehead and her left hand clipping together the two corners of Mother's towel, which she'd wrapped around her shoulders to protect them from dye.

"Oh god, Easter," The Mother moaned, "we're going to get the plague in here. Do you know what happens to people who spend more than fifteen minutes in a hospital bathroom? You don't wanna know. How's your head?"

"It feels fine."

"Good. Couldn't you have just waited ten more minutes before bonking your head on the table? We're going to get the measles in here. Or the flesh-eating virus. Goddammit, Easter, we're going to get the flesh-eating virus now. Do you know what that is?"

"I could make a pretty good guess, I think," said Easter.
"Don't be smart, young lady."

When the doctor finally called them in, he asked Easter a number of questions.

"What's the first thing you remember when you woke up?" was one of them.
"Julia," I said.
"Julia." He scribbled it down. "Who's Julia?" His eyes still down on his paper.

The Mother cleared her throat, an attempt to indicate to Easter that she should shut up about Julia, but Easter didn't realize that because she was still too young to know that sometimes people cleared their throats to get other people to shut up or change the subject or act differently than how they'd just been acting.

"Julia is my sister."
"Your sister?"
"Yeah."
"I didn't know you had a sister."
"That's because she doesn't," piped The Mother. "Julia is her . . . her imaginary friend, I guess you could call it."
"How old are you, Easter?"
"Eleven."
"Eleven, hm? That's a bit old for imaginary friends, isn't it?"

Before Easter could correct him, tell him that Julia wasn't imaginary, The Mother pried a spot for herself into the questioning:

"It's perfectly normal," she said.

"Is that a professional opinion?" The doctor seemed annoyed.

And The Mother went quiet again.

"So you see Julia all the time?"

"Not all the time. But most of the time."

"Like I'm standing here now?" the doctor continued.

The Mother wanted to intercept all of his questions, but he held a hand out to quiet her.

"Mm hmm." He nodded and scribbled and nodded and scribbled.

The doctor knew, now. He knew about The Lonely. Perhaps he could prescribe a Julia for The Mother, so that she wouldn't have to be lonely anymore either. Not that Easter wasn't lonely. She had it just like The Mother did, but Julia made it so much more bearable.

He suggested that they speak in private, he and The Mother. So they got up and left Easter alone. She sat high on the gray patient bed, moving her feet in circles, paper sheet crunching beneath her thighs. She hoped and hoped to the rhythm of her stirring feet that a Julia for The Mother came in an easy-to-swallow pill form.

While they were gone, Julia walked through the door. She'd put on a white coat and grabbed a clipboard from somewhere and imitated a doctor:

"Just as I suspected," she said in a deep voice, pretending to pore over the clipboard.

"What?"

"You're retarded."

Easter laughed and said, "Shut up, Julia."

"Seriously, though," Julia said, suddenly very serious, "I'm not feeling very well."

"What's wrong?"

Julia lifted the white coat and revealed a pattern of angry boils on her once-creamy thigh.

Easter recoiled slightly and said, "Julia, what did you do?"

"I don't know! There's this too, though."

And she pulled off a shoe to reveal a missing pinky toe.

"I think you've got the flesh-eating disease. The Mother said we could catch it in here."

"Ah fuck, Easter, you just had to go and whack your head."

"I'm sorry!"

"Well, I guess it'll be nice to have less body to worry about."

"That's awfully optimistic."

And then Julia coughed and gore splattered across the crispy clean sheet over the hospital bed. Easter picked up a chunk of it and squished it between her fingers.

"I'm no doctor, but I don't think this is a good sign," she said.

"No?" Julia laughed.

Then, with a crunch, she hoisted herself up next to Easter on the bed.

"They're talking about you in there, you know."

"They're talking about you, Easter."

"Well, yeah, but only because of you."

And suddenly The Mother stormed back into the room and pulled Easter off the bed and pulled her to the car. They never saw that doctor again. And Julia's flesh-eating-disease death was certainly her most gruesome.

The Feasts

The one thing that was typical of The Father, or at least of what I've seen of fathers on TV, is that he was painfully cheap. And this cheapness was like a powerful seasoning to him, or some kind of unique palatal mutation that allowed him to enjoy things that were about to turn rotten and tasted like feet. He could often be found in the kitchen, checking the labels of things deep in the recesses of the fridge, his folded, black-rimmed glasses held up to his face as he considered the date. Would it make him sick? If so, how sick? Would he pay the cost of said item to *not* vomit? This, he told me once, was the true determining question.

He would carefully arrange his feast on our kitchen table, which was wooden and blemished with deep gouges from where I used to grate the bottom of my spoons and knives and forks into it. Julia never did this. She was always a good eater. And to show for it she hadn't left a single mark on the table, not a gash or a scallop or even a bruise.

He would arrange the jars and containers into a little kingdom: castles of boxes and cartons and jugs with moats of opened salad dressings and jams emitting their own almost-salad-dressing or almost-jam-like smell, but not quite. No, everything was always noticeably off, even if only a little bit. He sat at the head of the table, the devouring king of all that lay before him.

I would sit with him for as long as I could stand watching him eat the stuff, finding the edible centers of things unrecognizable with mold or hard discolorations. Scraping and ripping and breaking things apart. It was because I sat there and insisted on bearing witness to his obsessive finishing off of things that I was served the nearly rotten pudding, which I refused to eat, which made him insist that I get a job and learn the value of a dollar, which is why he first suggested I work at the Miniature Wonderland with Mortimer Ungula. Mr. Ungula to you. And to me.

Mr. Ungula and the Miniature Wonderland

Mr. Ungula had hair that was always reacting rhythmically to his movements, like water carried in a too-small bucket. It was dense as a tongue and once, I swear, it lapped the end of his nose. Which is really quite a feat when you think about the size of Mr. Ungula's nose: a long, twisted affair with whiskery wrinkles running along the sides and up to the delicate inner corners of his eyes which were very brown and very wet and very twitchy like a pair of large squirrel noses. The bags under his eyes were loaded with flesh: pouches, soft and begging to be squeezed, the way that a baby's big soft cheeks urge you to stroke them.

A stripe of beard made a line down the center of his chin and curled at the end like a fiddlehead. He wore shiny shirts the whole year round, which pattered over with sweat in the summer and peeked from beneath tattered old blazers in the winter. His hands were all knuckle, fingernails embedded with dark model paint. He kept naked scotch mints in his pockets and sucked on them animatedly whenever he wasn't smoking the long brown cigarettes that he rolled himself on the back porch of the Miniature Wonderland.

It had been the Miniature Wonderland for as long as most people could remember, though everyone was aware, in one way or another, of its previous life as an army barrack. For one thing, it looked like a barrack: long and straight and window-less, straddling the perimeter of town. For another, it was the site of an often-whispered-about scandal involving an initia-tion ritual and an unlucky goat. Either way, as an army bar-rack or as the Miniature Wonderland, there it sat, in a pool of gravel parking lot overrun with grass, a front door on one end, and a porch built into the side toward the back.

The Father had become acquainted with Mr. Ungula at the music store. Not friends, mind you, just acquaintances. Both of them would remind me of that on my first day. They each played rather obscure instruments: The Father his clarinet and Mr. Ungula, I would come to learn, a large antique organ. Somehow during one of their conversations, The Father learned that Mr. Ungula owned the Wonderland. Bought it forty years ago from the city and had been working inside it, more or less alone, ever since. Over the past few years, how-ever, the barrack and Mr. Ungula had begun to age at the same pace, both reluctantly requiring more and more assis-tance all the time. And that's how I ended up with the job.

When I told Julia about it she was sitting upside down on the couch, her legs over the backrest and her head hanging and bloating with blood.

She laughed and said, "We're not getting a job, Easter."

"I know. I'm getting a job. Just me."

"What do you mean, just you?"

"I mean you're not allowed to come."

"Why not?"

"Because Dad said so," I lied.

"Easter, you're such an idiot."

"Why?"

"That was just about the worst lie I've ever heard."

"Okay fine, Julia, I don't want you to come because I don't wanna mess this up."

"Why? Because he got you the job?"

"Well, yeah, what's so bad about that?"

"Easter, he's not going to like you more just because you suck up to this weirdo friend of his. You can't do anything to make him like you more. He just doesn't like you and that's it."

"Weirdo acquaintance…" I muttered.

"What's that?"

"Nothing."

I wanted to tear her hair out, first with my hands and then with my teeth and not stop till her brains were showing.

"Pass me the mirror, please?" she asked.

So I did. And she covered the top part of her face so her chin looked like a head and she asked me to draw eyes on it and hair all the way down her throat.

I should take a minute to describe the Miniature Wonderland a little bit better. Mr. Ungula had separated the ex-barrack into four themed rooms depicting Our Town Over Time: Early Our Town, Later Our Town, Later Still Our Town, and Present Day Our Town, in order.

Most of the replicas covered the span of two wide dining room tables side by side, and Mr. Ungula took his time to make sure that every little detail was represented in every little room. Doors opened wide, cups could be raised to lips, leaves rustled, plants seemed to grow, and all of the appropriate documentation was represented: deeds to houses, permits for weapons, driver's licenses in wallets.

Mr. Ungula was always in the process of updating and adding to the Present Day Our Town model. For an hour each morning he would drive through town to make sure that everything was still the same. If something had changed, a banner at the used car dealership, a giant, inflatable gorilla in front of the mattress store for "We've Gone Bananas" month, Mr. Ungula would take a dozen pictures of it and adjust the Present Day Our Town model accordingly. Of course, by the time he finished the miniature alteration, the new thing had already been taken down and something newer erected in its place.

Mr. Ungula might have been the most detailed miniature

builder to ever walk the earth, but we'll probably never know because most miniature builders aren't really the competitive type.

The Miniature Wonderland was one of the quietest places I'd ever been. But it was an odd quiet. A recipe of constant little noises that imitated quietness: creaking floorboards, ticking clocks, a frame aching with age. Every nail and floorboard in the place still hard at work keeping the place together seemed to groan, a plea for some merciful meteor to smash it to death. But somehow the place seemed all the more quiet because of these sounds.

The only thing able to splinter the "silence" of the Wonderland was a loud train whistle that came from a station south of town. I'm not sure what was carried: people, livestock, explosives; but I did know that it blasted the Wonderland every day at twelve o'clock, three o'clock, and six o'clock. Twelve o'clock, three o'clock, and six o'clock.

The whistles seemed to bring light into the Wonderland, make it more clear, dust its shoulders, straighten its tie.

And Mr. Ungula would reset himself when he heard it. If he was getting very mad or frustrated or upset, when the whistle blew he became immediately composed, flattened the front of his shirt with one hand, and cleared his throat, a quick smile twitching into his face. Once I dropped a pot of paint into a filing cabinet, soaking a stack of miscellaneous papers in lime green. I thought he was going to kill me, sweat exploding from his pores, his skin shaking over his bones, but then the whistle blew and he relaxed. His pores sucked the sweat back in and his eyebrows unwound themselves. A hand slicked flat his hair, then off to the back porch to smoke it off.

He kept an immaculate log of the people who came in and out: how much money they spent, where they lingered, where they smiled, where they laughed, where they gagged, where they covered their children's eyes, where they stormed out, what they were wearing, how they smelled, the insults that a few scarred souls needed to hurl at him as they left, etc. Most often it was families: mothers or fathers, or both, with their children. Other times it was run-down middle aged women, some wearing Winnie-the-Pooh attire, pockets full of scratch tickets presumably, assisting or rolling their elderly parents through the tour. Sometimes a child accompanied, pushing an oxygen tank connected to their grandparent's nostrils.

I was the first spectacle of the tour, sitting like a rubber duck behind a round wood desk, paneled and ornamented with a sign that scrolled *RECEPTION* across its center. A cymbal-like lamp hung over my head from a long wire, which caused the dim, orange light to cascade into blackness in the corners of the room. I was instructed to smile, so I was smiling, and sometimes Mr. Harp the handyman smiled too; big and leaning in a dark doorframe, his pudgy triceps a cushion to his shoulder, causing fat to accordion up his neck all the way to his cheeks.

Mr. Ungula instructed me to write down the first things they said, how they reacted to the entrance fee, what they looked like, the acute change in atmosphere that accompanied them.

Day 9,321 (three customers):
The ugliest man alive came in today. He was as ugly as someone could possibly be before it's considered a real deformity or a disability even. Are people with severe facial deformities considered disabled? I wonder. His name: Peabody. His occupation: "Appreciator of fine things," he'd said. His face: A melting Clint Eastwood type. His mouth: A large, drooping frown weighted with heavy jowls. His smell: Musty, like a room once flooded, now drained and dried. His aura: Also drained and dried. His business: To examine Mr. Ungula's craft, write an article on it, submit it to a journal, and appear vicariously unique and creative for having found such genius and beauty in something so strange. The first thing he said to me was, "Well, aren't you just perfect."

The next customers to come in that day were a pair of young brothers. Probably close to my age. They both wore jeans and white T-shirts and were munching down Popeye Cigarettes to their ruddy fingertips as they spoke.

Names: Billy and Sol Hornburger. Occupations: Kids. Faces: Round and red. Aura: Also round and red. Smell: Coppery, sharp. Like park dirt and pennies and bloody noses. Business: "To check out the view," one had snickered. "Two please," the other said through wood chipper teeth, clouds of white, sugary dust billowing from the sides of his mouth as he inserted the candy smokes horizontally inward. "Ten bucks," I replied.

He slapped two fives on the table and took the key I handed him and they trampled off together through the first door. It was actually only four bucks, but I knew they'd come to peek at the naked women through some of the Our Town windows and for that the price doubled.

Mr. Ungula was uncommonly loud and very stubborn. He didn't believe in knocking on doors and butted his way through most of the Wonderland, announcing himself with a deliberately cleared throat seconds before he entered a room, which made you feel guilty about whatever you were doing even if it was something perfectly innocent.

He had seven sisters who called him many times a day, always worried about him or furious with him or trying to make him feel guilty. He spent a lot of time with his feet on his desk in his workshop, his head hanging backward over the top of his chair, one hand steadying the phone next to his ear, the other hand pulling down on his sallow cheek, exposing the red that cushioned his eyeball. I felt awful transferring the calls.

They were constantly setting him up with their friends and neighbors and manicurist's older sisters and their names were Nora, Nikki, Layla, Helen, Mona, Alice, and Brenda. Nora was the oldest and called him the most, Mona was the smartest and called him the least. When Nora called, she let out a yawn and encoded within it were the words, "Izzy in?" Just one yawn. And then she hung up as soon as the words "yes" or "no" left my mouth.

Nora liked to carry conversations with Mr. Ungula toward the subject of morality and then scream at him for being such a heathen. You see, Mr. Ungula didn't believe in marriage and had sympathy for pedophiles. When he read about either incident in the paper he would say, "Those poor sick bastards." Then flutter closed the newspaper and steal to the back porch to roll a cigarette.

When Nikki called I heard the flapping of her eyelashes, "Hi Esther, is my bruddadaya?" Her voice sounded pink, through wet, bubblegummy lips. I never corrected her about my name. It didn't seem worth the trouble.

Layla had six sons and she would command me to "put Morty on the phone."

Helen had six daughters and she would say, "Oh hello, Easter darling, how are you? Is my brother around? I hope he is this time, I wouldn't want to have to call again just to speak to my own brother, you understand. Isn't it funny? I was always Mortimer's favorite and now I have to fight to get a phone call with him. Is he there, sweetie? You can tell me, you know. I won't tell him you told me. But is he there? Just, shhh, don't tell me. I think I know."

Mona played softball and mumbled quietly into the phone, "HelloEastercanispeaktomybrotherplease?thankyou."

Alice and Brenda lived together and shouted at me through speakerphone. "Hey there, is he in?" one of them would squeal and the other would say, "Has Nora called?" "Yeah, did Nora call? What did she want?" I would tell them that I didn't know what Nora wanted, that she hadn't told me, she never does, she never speaks to me. And they would tell me that Nora was a bitch and never said thank you to anyone in her life, but not to tell Morty they said that, or Nora for that matter, but of course I wouldn't get the chance to tell Nora because she's such a bitch when she calls. Ha ha!

I liked to chat with Alice and Brenda from time to time, but they made Mr. Ungula the angriest. He would munch aspirin as they spoke over each other into his ear.

Julia hated when I was away at work and kept me up all night over it. Kicking me just when I fell asleep or pushing me out of bed. She even brought back a terrible dream that used to keep us up all night when I was small.

Bad Dreams

The whole thing flickers like an old newsreel. Sepia. Scars in the film crackling through the sky, black lightning through a bright white day. Easter is standing in the middle of a wide, grassy field. She is a beautiful girl. A naked girl. A girl who drinks in the sun voraciously. And the sun loves to be drunk by her, begs for it. You can feel it in the air, how much he loves to be consumed by her, his happiness making everything electric. Dripping down her chin, plopping to her chest, funneled by her protruding rib cage downwards, over the mound of her young belly and settling mostly in her navel, warming her whole body from there. And Easter is happy, so happy, and proud of her smoothness and countable bones. She belches sun and pats her stomach, satisfied.

A pair of eyes appear behind her, but she doesn't notice them.

Big, unblinking eyes. Blue and white and red, staring out from the precipice of the woods that surround the field.

Tall trees with tumorous trunks, their roots spread like patient dragon claws. Sounds of cold water coming from somewhere inside. A creek, perhaps: pulsing, eroding, scrambling over rocks.

And the eyes. Which sit side by side, irises facing forward, nestled in a deep scar along a fallen log. With their bottoms squeezed, wedged, into the bark, the tops of the eyes appear bigger and more bulbous than they probably are. But who knows what they'd looked like in a head. You can throw a pair of eyes onto anything and give it a personality. Just ask Officer Big Mac.

Knuckles of rocky earth jut from the ground, tall enough for a person to hide behind. Which, of course, there was. A person hiding. Because this is a dream, and there are always people crouching in the dark corners of dreams. In this dream, the person who'd left the eyes hides behind the largest wedge of rock, perched on his haunches like a frog, biting his fingernails down to the quick, not stopping till he tastes blood, then going further still, gnawing at them from the front with excitement; laying his heavy tongue against the raw, pink nail beds, hot and sore. Had they been his own eyes? One can't quite tell. Because although his face is fully visible, the dream makes it somehow difficult to see whether there are a pair of eyes in his head or just two empty sockets. Woven through with a metal ring, like the skirt of mink in The Cube.

Julia made us dream about that man a lot when we were small and again when I started leaving her to go to the Wonderland. Hiding somewhere in the creek woods, removing his eyes, resting them in bird's nests and in branches, seeing things he wasn't supposed to see. I'd started sleeping on the couch to get away from the dream but it didn't work; she still found me, made me bolt up straight and make my way upstairs.

But one night it was The Parents who woke me up, not the dream. They walked in, heavy footsteps, and I stole upstairs in a blink, unseen. Julia was already sound asleep under the covers, the top of her head peeking out, her hair a splash of moonlit red across my pillow. I crawled in next to her, let our spines grate against one another; our bodies curved and tucked up like a pair of open butterfly wings against the sheet.

A few minutes later the tops of our heads were pushed right up against one another, our ears pressed to the floor. I liked the feeling of the top of Julia's head on my head. Our two hard skulls pressed together, adjusting and re-setting against each other's little dents and deformities. Our hair scraped together like sandpaper and thundered in my ears. Things sound quite different when they come from above your head.

Ours was the hottest room in the summer and the coldest room in the winter due to a pair of badly warped window frames next to the closet. There were many microscopic breaches in our room through which harsh, angry winds turned to whispers, and it was at one of these tiny fissures, a small violation between two floorboards, that Julia and I huddled, warming our ears on the reverberations of The Parents' screaming.

It was a stifling hot night in July. The heartbeat of an old ceiling fan lub-dubbed above our heads, moving the air heavily like a spoon through stew. We were both in long white tank tops, loose with the memory of a few hours sleep. I don't think that Julia thought at all about our heads rubbing together. Touching me wasn't the moment, the thrill, the delight that it was for me to touch her.

The Parents were fighting about the bells. The Mother sobbing hard, incapable of catching her breath, saying that she needed them, that it relaxed her to hear how we moved through the house. The Father, anger growing steadily warmer like a stove-top coil, insisted that she had no right.

     "I hate the bells," Julia whispered.
     "Really? I don't even notice them."
     "Honestly, Easter, sometimes I wonder why I've bothered with you."
     "What do you—"
     "Shh, I want to hear this."

My knees were starting to hurt. I wriggled my splayed-out fingers a bit and stretched one leg out, then the other, then I moved back on my haunches and looked at Julia's face. It's harder to hear someone when their head is pressed up against yours; two layers of skull and brain instead of just one rubs words down into mumbles.

     "Why do you hate the bells?" I asked her.

I didn't mean to but I'd let a little bit of venom creep into the question, slowly, in reaching tendrils, like the blood that replaces medicine in a syringe. I didn't like that she hated them so much and I didn't.

"Because they're terrible, Easter. It changes a person to hear bells all the time."

"What do you mean?"

"People use bells to train animals; don't you know that? The Mother is training us."

"For what?"

"To be just like her."

"I don't understand."

"Yeah, that's what I'm worried about."

"She's not training me."

"She is, and it's already working."

"What do you mean?"

"You're leaving me behind."

"Julia—"

"SHH! I'm trying to hear!"

So I put myself back on my hands and knees and pushed my head once again against Julia's.

But they'd moved into the living room where we couldn't quite make out the words. Where all that passed up through our floorboards were the guttural depths of The Mother's sobs, the sound of her lungs snapping back after almost folding in on themselves she was crying so hard. And The Father might not even be on the main floor anymore. He might have retired to the basement, through with the conversation because he knew he didn't have to fight with her if he didn't want to. He knew that she would never leave him no matter what he did. But she was still crying hard, still talking to someone. It scared me that she might be all alone, talking to herself in the living room.

And for a minute I really hated The Mother. Hated her for how pathetic she was. Hated her for making me pathetic too. I wanted to be rid of her. I felt as though if she were gone I would be a much better person. Not better in a way like I'd start volunteering or giving things to charity or anything like that, but better in the way that I'd be more beautiful and happier and more confident and be able to speak easily to big groups and impress everyone. She was like a shell I'd outgrown, that I needed to crack and peel off of me and emerge as the thing I really was. But the more I thought about how much I hated her, the sicker I felt. The guiltier. The more sure I was that I needed to get rid of her for good.

The basement bell rang loud. The sound made me think of burying my fist into The Mother's stomach, kitchen knife first.

And the guilty nausea wouldn't stop. I just wanted to lie in bed and simmer with the rest of the air in the room. I would be a tuber if our room were a stew. I stood up and made my way to our bed.

"Hey, where are you going?" Julia looked up at me with big confused eyes.

"I'm going to bed."

"Why? They might start up again. Please stay up, Easter. Come on."

"No."

"Why not?"

"Because we can't hear anything anyway, Julia." I lifted the thin sheet and crawled beneath. "And my knees hurt. And I'm tired. And I hate what I'm thinking about so I'm going to go to bed."

Julia's eyes narrowed to whiskers and she hissed at me through thin lips:

"Goddammit, Easter, you're no fun at all."

She stood up, stomped over to the bed, flung up the sheet as loudly as you can possibly fling up a sheet, and smashed down onto the mattress beside me. Her anger made her bigger and more cumbersome to sleep with than usual. She pulled the covers over to her side gradually and almost completely, daring me to say something about it. I shivered until I knew she was asleep and gently pulled some back to my side.

Miniature Wonderland,
Day 9,330 (One Customer)

A boy with a long neck and hunched shoulders, his head mounted on his body like a stuffed deer head to a wall. Like he's spent most of his life crammed into a box, or a cave, growing into its constricted dimensions. Long brown hair falling over one eye, a kink running through it like a recently unfolded sheet. Large ears with soft-looking lobes, warm hanging honey. Sweet. White T-shirt accentuating a small frame, yellow under the armpits, a hole along the seam, a peek at barely opaque skin. Maybe he's lived his whole life in a cave, tucked away from sunlight. He doesn't move his arms as he walks; they hang still at his sides like a suspended axolotl's.

As he approached my reception desk I wanted to run away, heart fluttering as hard as a trapped bird. I was scared of him.

"Hello," he said.

I knew he was going to say it but it startled me anyway.

Then he said, "I'm sorry for scaring you. How much to go through?"

I pointed to a sign behind me. He nodded.

"I'm Easter," I blurted. I'm Easter and I'm an ass who lets nonsense fly from her mouth.

"I'm Lev."

"I have to find out your name so that I can fill out your particulars in this book here. It's got everyone's particulars."

"Particulars."

Particulars? I wanted to fix the barrel of a gun to each of my eyeballs and blow my brains out in either direction. Particulars. Mr. Ungula's idiotic words coming out of my mouth.

"Yeah, your information. Your specifics."

"Well, my name is Lev. And I've seen you before, walking through the woods in town."

"Oh?" I'd heard ladies say it in movies like that: *"Oh?"* I didn't really know how someone was supposed to respond to it, but it seemed appropriate here. I waited to see what he'd do with it.

"Yeah. I saw you there. And then I followed you here."

"You followed me?"

"I did. You seemed wonderful to me."

I seem wonderful to him. I opened my eyes wide. Wonderful. Wonderful. He seems wonderful to me, for thinking that I'm wonderful. I might not have found him wonderful until he thought I was wonderful. And the sound of the bells filled my ears, loud and warm and vibrating. Julia would kill me if she heard this. Kill me even harder if she could feel how happy I was in this moment that she was gone. And then I felt terribly guilty; it moved through me slow as oil, coated my insides like Pepto-Bismol does in the commercials. Thick pink guilt. Now that I knew he thought I was wonderful, I wasn't nervous anymore. My heart sucked in the wings it had momentarily grown. I'm wonderful, so who cares. The bells quieted a bit but didn't go away.

"Well, are you going to go through or not?"

My sudden impatience caused his neck to droop further.

"What's the rush?" he said.
"If you're not going to buy a pass you've gotta leave. Those are the rules."
"I don't have any money," he said.

And I shrugged, not really wanting him to leave and not really knowing why I was being so mean. He left quietly, leaving two little insects behind where he'd stood. Had they fallen from him? Maybe he really did come from underground, crawled from a grave just to tell me I was wonderful.

These are his "particulars" in the book:
Name: Lev

Occupation: Boy
Aura: Cramped and sore, grown too much without enough room. The see-through skin and red-rimmed eyes of a blind cave newt. Axolotl arms. A bit wonderful, too.
Smell: Dry skin and peppermint chewing gum.
Business: To tell me that I'm wonderful.

Lev. Lev. Lev. Long Lev. The Long Necked Lev. Once trapped in a box, a water dragon in an aquarium, but now free to roam the Miniature Wonderland. I thought about chewing on Long Lev's honey-dripped earlobes, spreading them on crackers to eat. The way I'd once thought about Julia's lips, as spreadable and delicious. But the bells didn't ring encouragement when I thought about eating Julia's lips the way they did when I thought about eating Lev's ears. Maybe this meant I was getting normal.

A Bad Day

The Father spent most of his time down in the basement and decorated it in all the stuff that was a little too good to throw out but not nice enough to keep on the middle, our most presentable, floor.

A grimy fish tank, once occupied by an ill-fated party of gold-fish, was now turned upside down and used to hold a small television. An ancient set, infected with a virus of off-color distortion that spread slowly and steadily from the bottom left-hand corner. The Father would watch the news down there; I could hear it muffled through the floor. Across from that, a big blue worn-out corduroy chair with crops of patches all over it from Denmark, Amsterdam, wherever. I think it was supposed to look like it had been all over the world, but really it just came from a Sears in Michigan and it was one of the ugliest chairs I'd ever seen. We called it "The Everywhere Chair." He had a computer down there too, an old one with a big, heavy monitor and a grubby keyboard.

He also had a couple of old clarinets. He used to play in the band when he was in high school and sometimes I would sit at the top of the basement steps and listen to him playing "When the Saints Go Marching In" or some other high school band favorite. I pictured him with his full band-member uniform on: big black boots and a tasseled gold-trimmed hat on top of his head. But I'm pretty sure that he wasn't wearing that. What was more likely was that he was sitting up straight in the well-traveled chair, his bare feet flat on the floor and facing outward. There would be an open window and an ashtray next to it, a cigarette burning down, snuggled into one of the specifically designed grooves along the side. Its smoke blew straight out the window, as though it had been directed beforehand as to where it should make its exit. He might be wearing his robe and he was definitely squishing one eye shut.

I sat at the top of the stairs a lot, trying to hear what he could possibly be doing down there all the time. I wanted to learn something, anything, about him. Maybe even find something I could use to interest him. He might be breeding iguanas down there. If he was, then I could become an expert on crickets and help him find the best possible type of cricket to use to keep his iguanas strong and healthy. Then, when he sold them for lots of money, he would have me to thank.

Now we had Mr. Ungula. A mutual friend, a personality we could both comment on, share and criticize and laugh about. But we didn't.

Sometimes The Mother would kneel down next to me and

ruffle my hair with her hand, letting it linger for a few seconds on my warm skull, then use it stand up straight again and walk away. A few times she brought me snacks while I sat there. Quiet things like pudding or buttered white bread with sugar and cinnamon on top. Often I would occupy myself with Tetris, putting it on mute so that I could still hear. Only she could know how terrible it was to want someone like him.

The Father makes a decent amount of money at a regular type of job at which he stays late, sometimes all night, and he has a secretary who's always writing notes for him on slips of blue paper. The last time I was at his office I had to hoist myself up onto my tiptoes and make whites of my knuckles to look over the desk at what she was doing: filling out a list of appointments for June 16th. Her nails were long and scratched softly against the paper as she wrote in black ink. She was the kind of person who had a hard time looking people in the eyes.

I'd once heard him say that he was just about the most bored person who'd ever lived.

It used to be that we ate dinner together. And The Parents would fight and we'd go on drives to get ice cream or feed the ducks in the park and he'd hold my hand crossing streets and she would wear short skirts and pretty blouses and he would pinch the skin above her wrist. But something happened. And they stopped talking to one another and I ended up on The Mother's side, somehow, while she unfolded slowly, her insides on the outside so she was nothing but a big fat sore: tender and infected and wincing and painful to be near. But she loved everyone so much that she couldn't be alone. And he hated us so much that he couldn't be near us at all. And I hated him for it, so I wanted to bother him. But actually I didn't. I didn't hate him at all. I loved him so much that I hated myself for it. And it was all her fault for making me this way.

The upstairs of our house was even more strange; urgent with the smell of overripe pears all soft and grainy and sopping. About to turn, anxious to be eaten. Wetness settled in corners, curdled the floorboards and boiled the walls so bubbles expanded beneath the dark green paper, all transformed by the greasy heat of The Mother's hot Sunday tubs.

But the upstairs didn't belong to The Mother the way that the downstairs belonged to The Father. It wasn't shut off, or made exclusively hers somehow. There was just something very distinctly *Mother* about it. Something private and close to her. The steam of her broth lingering in the air, a visible vapor, like a cartoon smell with a mind of its own, the taste of bath oils and talc all through your mouth and lungs.

We were all welcome up there, stairs wide open and inviting, a small, bare window spilling sunlight over the foyer. Dust emblazoned and twinkling in the rays. Almost too welcoming. Like the witch's cottage in the woods. It might have been this dangerous openness that warped the paper on the walls.

And though it was too welcome to us, it wasn't at all welcome to outsiders. Whenever she found out that someone had been to our house, Phyllis usually, Amelia once, or from time to time a friend of The Father's, she always asked, with air trapped, suspended in her lungs like a note, "They didn't go upstairs, did they?" to which I would respond, "No, of course not." And then she would exhale, a shallow, nervous cloud of cracked breath. A hand on her chest, relief on her face. No one could be allowed to see. Our house wasn't like the houses in sitcoms.

One afternoon The Mother's voice sliced into the middle floor. Our most presentable pulp.

> "Easter!"
> "Eaaaaaaster!"
> "EAAAAAAAAASTER!
> "WHAT?" I screamed in reply.
> "Can you come upstairs please?"

I was often angry on Sunday afternoons because it meant that I'd lost bathroom access. Or rather, she'd deprived me of it. Either way, I couldn't satisfy my mirror habit. The Mother would be in there all night long, soaking up the heat from her bathwater until it was ice cold and then starting over again. Hours.

Often she called me up to sit with her, which was a horrible tease. I indulged in the thought of pulling her out of the tub, throwing her slippery into the hallway, and locking the door. Then I'd wrap my head in a towel and scream until I puked. I hated not having that mirror all day. To press my face against and stare at.

In a massive angry motion I grabbed my bandana from the couch cushion next to me, where I had been sitting playing Tetris for the past couple of hours. I wrapped it around my face and tied it tight in the back. This should be fine.

The air became warmer as I grumbled up our wooden stairs, which made sounds to echo my exasperation. I opened the bathroom door, bringing a puff of cooler hallway air in with me.

"Easter?" she said.

The shower curtain was closed around the tub; she rattled it open with the backside of her hand and her eyes flicked to my bandana. A barely audible twitch in her throat shivered its way to her bottom lip, betraying that she wanted to say something about it, some criticism or concern. But she didn't. Instead, she smiled.

I could tell she'd been playing her favorite tub game: sitting as quiet and still as a mouse, trying her best to trick the water into thinking that no one was in it. She would sit with her head against the side of the tub, oddly cocked forward so that she could look down at the rest of her body, which was skewed and made to look strange by the movement of the water. She would look down at herself with her lips pursed, held in deep concentration, staring accusingly at the minute ripples which betrayed that there was a living, moving body in there.

The Mother was a beautiful lady, that's for sure. But she didn't share any of those genes with me. She used up all the good stuff on Julia and left me with the scraps. I was forced to pick through the bargain bin of man genes that The Father had to offer. Not that he was disgusting, really, but in girl form he was kind of disgusting. Which I'm proof of.

The Mother had a precious smile. And a lovely nose, sort of squared-off at the end like a tiny toy dice. Her face was a series of crisp lines, sharp cheeks and a high forehead. She was meticulous about her skin and it showed, glowing in a moonlit sort of way. Her hair was blonde and straight as an arrow. Her body long and graceful even when she was laden with groceries. Most of the time I was excessively, psychotically jealous of her. But The Mother loved me so shamelessly much that I felt guilty about it. It was like being jealous of your dog because he gets to sleep in.

>"Yeah, I'm here."
>"What were you doing down there?"
>"Just playing Tetris."
>"Well, do you think you could play it up here for a while?"

I transformed the action of putting down the toilet seat lid and sitting on it into a kind of irritated affirmative. What I really wanted to do was implode. Be sucked up in a hiccup of smoke, any trace of me inhaled by the muggy bathroom air. Not that I necessarily wanted to die, just to stop existing in that exact second.

She looked at me and smiled, her face sticky. I pulled the bandana off my face.

"Just so you know, I'm not responding to yelling anymore," I said.

Her smile disappeared.

"What? Why?"

"Because it's not civilized, Mom. Normal people don't scream at each other like that."

"But you screamed at me. You screamed, 'What?'"

"That's because it's how I was raised. I can't help it."

"Oh Easter, that doesn't seem fair."

I shrugged.

With my elbows on my knees, I resumed the game of Tetris I'd started on the couch. I wondered if she'd noticed the Game Boy. The Mother has this every-other-year-or-so habit of suddenly being overwhelmed by the clutter in our house. She'd get this horribly suffocated look on her face and begin indiscriminately strong-arming piles of books and papers and toys into hearty black garbage bags. Julia and I would have to chase after her and pull from her claws those things that absolutely had to stay. The Game Boy just barely made it a couple of years ago.

Those things that linger too long unused, that find themselves settling into the cracks and corners of a house so familiar to its inhabitants as to become invisible, neglected toys and fridge magnets and oversized paper clips and cereal box treasures, all suddenly stood out to The Mother like blood stains. She hated the sight of things not touched, wearing the dusty evidence of their loneliness like a coat. She said she couldn't relax, but I think it was more than that. The clutter made her scared. Uncomfortable. Like it might not realize that she wasn't part of it and make her invisible too.

I must have seemed all settled in because The Mother exhaled in a satisfied way. I guess she'd decided to take a little break from concentrating on her dead body. I suppose everyone needs a break. She had me now, at least for a short while, and you could tell she was happy to have another body in the room.

> "Easter's Feature. If you ever open up a restaurant or a movie theater or something, that's what it should be called. Easter's Feature. I could see myself going there, or at least telling people that that's where I was going."
>
> "I'll keep it in mind, I guess."
>
> "You'll forget it. But I'll remind you if you ever call me up and tell me that you're opening a family type restaurant, or a drive-in. Now that's a good idea: a drive-in. I think it's just about time for a drive-in theater to do well again. It's in the vault, kiddo! I've got a vault full of good ideas for you."

"Thanks, Mom."

"Not a problem, Easter. You're lucky because you've got two people working on your life. Me and you. A lot of people only have themselves to figure things out."

I tried to remember the last time she'd actually helped me out, wanted in fact to ask her when she felt as though she'd been helpful to me in any way, but I held back because I knew she was being sincere. I'd let her have this moment to relax. It wouldn't last long. I could already feel a fight foaming in my guts. Hateful things that I wanted to unleash on her at some point today. There was something about her, maybe that wide openness which curdled the walls, that made it so easy to be mean to her. That made me want to hurt her so badly.

"How was school last week?"

Her eyes were closed and she had stretched her neck along the height of the tub. The plastic, nautically themed shower curtain was pulled open and tied to the wall with a hearty white rope.

"It sucked."

"That's a disgusting word, Easter. Sucked. Sucked what, that's what I want to know. There is something very nasty implied there."

I rolled my eyes.

"Anyway, I'm sure it wasn't that bad."

Her breathing was evening out, becoming shallower. She was preparing herself for another bout of stillness.

I returned once again to my Tetris, feeling irritated that all she could come up with to ask me was, "How was school?" I replaced the bandana over my face and jabbed the buttons on the Game Boy a little harder than I should have. It was an antique, after all.

"And how are you feeling lately?" she asked.

She'd closed her eyes and stretched up her neck like an ostrich.

"What do you mean?"

"I mean, how are you feeling? Is there anything you want to talk to me about? Any questions you might have of someone as old and wise as I am?"

She smiled very gently, careful not to move her neck too much. She always asked me these very annoying and obvious questions. She told me that talk shows told her it was her job to ask me questions like that. I told her I was special and that those questions didn't apply to me and she laughed and said, "I know Easter." What I didn't add was that it was Julia who made me special. That I had Julia working with me, not The Mother. And in fact I didn't want The Mother's help anyway.

"Mothers should really stop doing whatever talk shows tell them to do. Because apparently talk shows don't realize how annoying it makes them."

My words, all muffled and warm beneath the bandana, smelled sour and angry. The Mother scowled.

"When are you going to throw out that disgusting bandana?" she asked.

I shrugged.

"You shouldn't have it on your face like that, Easter. It will give you pimples."
"Mmm hmm."

I agreed in a way that made her think I wasn't listening, but I was listening, and later I'd scrub my face raw.

She lay still, with the shower curtain wide open. After a little while the scowl melted from her face and her breathing became perfectly even. The water moved very slightly back and forth, back and forth, coming slowly to almost a complete stop. The Mother hadn't moved a muscle, even her chest, in minutes, and the only thing bringing life to the water at all was the vibration of her blood pulsing through her heart and body. I looked at her hands, open at her sides, empty, aware, not laden with the heavy nothingness which fills dead or sleeping hands.

I didn't want her to fall asleep in there. At least, that's why I told myself I knocked over The Father's electric shaver so it smashed onto the floor in an explosion of jagged bits of plastic and exposed metal. Really, I wanted to see her cry. The Mother screeched and leapt so high in the air that I thought she might cling to the ceiling like a cat. Her eyes wide open, arms hooked over the lip of the tub; water splashed all over the floor.

"Easter, what the hell was that?"

She was breathing heavily and staring me in the eyes, my face telling her nothing beneath the bandana. I pointed at the shaver in pieces on the floor.

The Mother's jaw dropped, her cheeks grew red.

"Oh Easter, no. No, no, no. Not his razor, honey."

Her face was the kind that moved to tears slowly, as though a key was turning somewhere in her brain, tightening, grinding.

And I knew that it would make her cry. I knew that she would dread having to give The Father the bad news. I knew that it would reinforce all of the terrible things he already thought about me. Which were all true. And I felt awful about it. But I wasn't going to say that. Easter, you're an evil, fat little bitch.

She rolled back over into the tub. Little waves were moving the water back and forth with her under them, grabbing at her plump cords of wet hair dangling just above the surface.

The water now knew there was something very much alive in it.

That night Julia and I lay in bed, staring out the window. The sky looked like stretched fabric. So dark as to actually be there. I thought of the time she was crushed in The Cube. That I'd been the one who crushed her, really, when I pulled the book from the wall of stuff. I thought about Lev coming by again yesterday, and how he'd brought his cigarettes and we smoked them in the parking lot and I flicked a bug off his shoulder. The first time I'd touched him. And he was real, I could tell. Not something crawled out of the ground, despite the bugs and the filmy eyes. He asked me again if I'd ever had a boyfriend. And for the first time ever, I told the truth and said "No." And he smiled and said that he'd never had a girlfriend either. I wanted to say that I wasn't surprised because he was a gooey-looking, thin-skinned subterranean humanoid, but I didn't. He'd been coming by a lot since I first took down his particulars, but Julia didn't know that.

"I know what you're thinking," Julia said.

"No you don't."

"I do. You're thinking you want to kill me."

"Julia, I am not."

"You are, Easter. How come?"

"I don't know."

"Why don't you want me around anymore? Don't you love me?"

"Julia, I love you more than anything. You're my best and only friend. You know that."

"Then why won't you let me come to work with you? And why are you thinking about killing me?"

"I don't know. I've gotta get un-lonely, Julia. Un-lonely for real. You make me do and think awful things sometimes. You wanted to cut up Amelia. I knew you meant it, Julia. And you can make me do things. And—"

"You're a psycho."

"That's what I'm trying to tell you!"

"No, not like that, Easter. You don't want to be special anymore. That's psycho. We could have a different life from everyone else."

"Is that really better, though?"

She shook her head and looked at me, making a face like she was amazed at my stupidity. I tucked the covers under my chin and snuggled closer to her. I could feel her words move along her body before I heard them.

"Remember when you killed Salty?"

"You killed Salty."

"You don't really believe that, Easter."

"I didn't kill him."

"Then who did?"

"You."

Salty was a cat that belonged to Seisyll, our unfriendly neighborhood cat man. He chewed tobacco and spit into a brown bottle and was always trailed by as many as eight cats at a time, meowing and spitting and stinking. His house sat at the crux of our gaping cul-de-sac, a feast for ivy and weeds and a creeping stench.

One afternoon Salty strayed from Seisyll and sidled his way up to Julia. She'd been making a game of pulling off never-ending strings of ivy stems that had suctioned themselves to the red brick steps of The Tooth House.

He performed a little pre-sit ritual, three full circles, and then plopped his butt down next to her. His tail stuck out straight as an arrow, hiding that nasty balloon end that other cats always seem so eager to show off, and it made him seem more respectable somehow. His modest butthole, coupled with a little piece of frayed grass that hung from his lip like a cigar, made him one of the most distinguished little gentlemen she'd ever met. Then he got up and slid down the steps and smelled her sandaled feet and grated her toes with his rough little tongue. She pulled a red ribbon from her hair, tied it around his neck, and coaxed him easily to the lawn, where she pulled up dandelions and bopped his nose with them, sending him into a tizzy of jumping and batting. By the time she decided it was time to take him home, his nose was almost completely yellow.

When night came and it was time to go inside, she felt awful to leave him all alone. She wanted to return him to Seisyll's house but didn't want to walk up and knock on Seisyll's door. So instead she lifted the plastic lid of Seisyll's garbage can at the end of his long driveway, which lolled like a tongue from his open garage, and poured Salty in. He hit the bottom with two gentle thuds, looked up at her, the ribbon still in a perfect bow. The shadow of the lid in her hand sliced little Salty in half vertically and one of his eyes flashed like a crystal ball.

"You left him in that garbage pail, Easter."

"No."

"You let him bake like a turkey in that August heat wave."

"I did NOT!" I screamed, and imagined pulling the pillow out from beneath her head, shoving it over her face, and feeling the life spill in violent glugs from her body like a tipped bottle.

Easter Story

Through two doors, The Mother sat and the girls watched. Easter's door was pushed open just a sliver, peeled from the frame as quietly as an eyelid opens. Light broke into their room and the burnt orange of a heavy lampshade painted their faces, stacked one on the other like a totem pole.

Easter was trying very hard to make herself invisible. Not only from The Mother, who couldn't see them from where she sat anyway, but also from Julia. She wanted to be as inconspicuous to Julia as a mint in her pocket. An accessory hanging from her ear or neck or wrist. A ghost. So that Julia would invite her to tag along again on another of these most secret excursions. Excursions she usually took alone, leaving Easter to mope in silent pretend sleep in their cold bed.

The pulled-back hairs on Julia's head felt as thick as wire along Easter's pulsating throat; nervous warmth billowed between them. Julia was as anxious as Easter was, to be spying so seriously in the dark.

Through two doors and across the width of the hall, The Mother looked stiff. Her legs were stuck together at the knees and she'd burrowed her hands flat beneath her thighs against the wood chair, which sat without any real use against the wall of The Parents' bedroom. Her feet hung by their heels on a round rung between the legs of the chair and her long, gray nightshirt looked damp and pulled around the neck. She stared at the spot where the girls knew that the bed was but couldn't quite see because the staggered placement of the two door frames only gave them that chair. But they knew she was looking at the bed. And they knew that the source of the dim, orange light was a ceramic table lamp with a woman's face painted onto it. Created by The Mother when she took up painting, then put the hobby in a box and shoved it under the bed with the rest of her neatly compartmentalized, barely realized interests.

On her face a Lonely expression was lacquered.

Through two doors, everything was silent except for the sound of The Mother's finger joints nervously bending and flattening with a thud against wood, trapped between the chair and her enveloping thighs. It was hard to tell whether or not The Father was on the bed; hard because on her face that Lonely expression was lacquered and because Julia said she sat like this most nights whether he was there or not. Quietly in the chair, legs as stiff as bent drinking straws, back as straight as she could make it, looking at the bed, her eyes cavernous: like two empty rooms, side by side, made up for viewing and not living. Vacant suites and dinette sets prepared for "The Price is Right" showcase showdowns.

Just as Julia began to indicate that they should head back to bed, The Mother stood up, smoothed the gray nightshirt down over her underwear, and walked to where the girls knew a dresser existed. The faint squeal of a drawer pulled out. Shuffling through things worn soft. Then The Mother returned to the chair with a cigarette and a holographic hula girl lighter in her hand. She opened the window, a fraction of which was visible to the girls across the hall and between the door frames; sat down again; and proceeded to operate the lighter very strangely: the holographic hula girl standing up straight in her cupped hand, wedged into her palm with the wheel under her middle finger. Then she pulled down and ignited it, and it looked as though the flame was coming straight from her first two fingers like magic.

As far as the girls knew, The Mother didn't smoke. Perhaps they'd seen her once or twice with a cigarette in her hand, at a party or some other function where it might look interesting to be the kind of person who sometimes smoked, but in real life never. This must have been a cigarette from one of The Father's secret stashes.

The Mother took two purposeful-looking drags from it, just to get the thing going, not really enjoying it. She pulled a leg up onto the chair and rested her arm over her knee, soft side up. One foot remained clipped to the chair rung beneath and the white underwear she'd made an effort to hide when she'd first stood up was now fully exposed to us. The warmed, private part of the underwear, scooped into with leg holes. A small embroidered bell in front.

She took another hungry drag and let the smoke slip from between her lips slowly, crawling up her face toward the ceiling, obscuring it for a second almost completely. Another drag she blew out gently against the inside of her arm. It moved along the soft inner parts like gentle, tickling fingers. Her skin must have rippled, hairs standing on end, because when she proceeded to move the burning end of the cigarette as close as she could along her arm, just barely above the skin along the pit of her elbow, the girls could smell burning hair.

Easter became frantic. What if she put the cigarette too close, buried the burning orange end into her most tender flesh, let herself eat up and put out the straight white cigarette with her doughy insides? The Mother's head rolled back, her throat as exposed as a fish on land, not looking at where she was moving the cigarette, just letting it hover above her skin. Easter began to tremble and Julia, who could feel the tremble ripple through her own body, shot an angry look up at her. This angry look made Easter shake even more. Julia wasn't going to stop her. Julia was just going to let her burn. And Julia wasn't going to let Easter stop her, either. A whimper escaped from Easter's until-now-vigilantly-monitored throat and Julia stood up like a shot, knocking Easter backward. She grabbed her by the wrist and dragged her back to bed without a word.

Easter secretly hoped that The Mother had heard them and that it knocked her out of it. She hoped that The Mother would throw the cigarette out the window and go to sleep whether The Father was there or not. Regardless of what The Mother did with that cigarette, Easter would never be invited on a secret excursion again.

In their room, Julia paced.

"Easter," she said, "do you mind telling me what's wrong with you? What makes you so, so annoying?"

Easter sat on the bed, looking at a section of Care Bear sheet through her crossed legs. Numb fingers, dry throat, fear and sadness and strangeness all vibrating through her, just beneath the skin. The small light in the room reflected a slick of tears across her cheeks.

"Hello?" Julia waved a hand in her face.

"I can't believe we just left her there," Easter said quietly.

"We didn't just leave her there, Easter, you made a noise. Now she knows we were watching. She's stopped."

"Do you think so?"

"I do."

"I hope so."

"And that's why you're not coming out with me again."

"Why?"

"Because you can't handle it, Easter. It's not right for you to see. Only I can, got it? From now on, you've got to never leave your room at night, all right? Even if you hear the bells or you wake up and see that I'm not there."

"Okay."

"Do you promise me?"

"Yes. I promise."

"I'll protect you from them."

"I know."

Footage

I used to be very mad at The Parents for never taking any home videos of me. There are a few pictures, but not many, and certainly none of all of us together. I wasn't mad because I particularly wanted to look at them or have them to show to my own kids or anything; I was mad because I took it as a sign that I would probably never be famous. Famous people always seem more worthy of documentation, even when they're little and packing wet sand into buckets at the beach, or in the high school band, hidden beneath a layer of greasy hormones. People around want to trap that specialness in a picture like a firefly cupped between two excited hands, peeking at it through the cracks in their fingers as the light begins to weaken.

And when the news wants to do a story on the girl who bled to death under a rock in the local woods, they won't have any good footage or pictures to use for the segment. This made me mad. They'll probably have to put my goddamn yearbook picture up there, full-faced too-freckly Richard

Nixon, appearing in a little box to the left of the newscaster's head. People will squint and wonder if it's a boy.

I began to seethe at the thought of it.

Until I remembered that everyone who dies young is remembered as beautiful and I'll be more popular as a corpse than I ever was alive. All of this blood spilled out over The Woods will soak everyone's memory, absorbed like a cotton ball until thoughts of me can only be recognized by my death. I won't be that weirdo who used to sit behind you in math. I'll be that lovely girl who died in The Woods with all of those wonderful troubles. And Lev will never get the chance to find out how truly un-wonderful I am.

The ground grew warm around me as the sun rose over the rock, for a split second a searing white thumbnail, brightness too much to bear. I squeezed my eyes shut. And they had to stay that way for a while. The ground simmered, leaves and twigs and pebbles as alive as droplets on a hot pan. Little bugs burrowing to the top, fat bees pollinating low flowers, all heavy and drunk with fertility. My bare skin roasting. The Mother would hate to see all of this sun on my face. Wrinkles and freckles seemed to terrify her in a way that drug addiction and teen pregnancy terrified other mothers. She had no reason to worry in that department, and she knew it. No one at school would have ever offered me drugs or sex.

I felt nervous with my eyes closed beneath the rock. Nervous that the scribble of invisible things surely collecting in the odor of my rotting legs would start to lay eggs in and around them before I was all the way dead. The air surrounding me was all excited and foaming with the microscopic matter that thrived on that sort of thing, a signal for bigger critters and feeders and parasites, nighttime creatures who had probably already smelled a bleeding body in The Woods, had already been watching anxiously from their shadowy hiding spots. With my eyes closed, they could begin to fantasize about the ways in which they would devour me when the sun finally went under. Rubbing their claws together hungrily, *slouching slightly closer*. Perhaps they're what scared the squirrel. Perhaps they're only waiting until dark to start feasting.

And the whole woods transformed behind my closed eyelids. The trees were stretching their limbs, arching their trunks, cracking their twigs, preparing for another length of stillness. The Woods filled with the sound and smell of their resounding exhalation, their warm, musky tree-breath invading my lungs: bronchiole branches, alveoli buds.

I heard a rustling of leaves behind me, somewhere behind the creek, the sound of feet sloughing off a layer of forest floor. A careless pair of feet from the sounds of it. Phyllis the Fucking Bitch always insisted that we raise our feet when we walked, so Julia and I had a good ear for shuffling.

With my eyes closed I heard the feet shuffle and shuffle, growing louder and louder until they suddenly stopped, as though they had caught a whiff of being heard. And their nervous stillness was even louder than their shuffling. My heart began to pound. I wanted desperately to open my eyes but it was still too bright to bear; my sockets were becoming little ovens, eyeballs broiling. I heard the sound of sniffing; erratic sniffing, the way that dogs do it.

I think even the trees stopped breathing.

What could this shuffling something be? Is it something coming to save me? Or something coming to finish me off? Or maybe I'm already dead, eyes as still as marbles on a carpet, and the something shuffling, The Something Coming, is a big dirty vulture coming to pierce my bloated belly with its beak, squawking the dinner bell to everything else in The Woods. I hope The Something Coming doesn't turn out to be me, walking along a path like I was this morning and somehow this whole thing turns into a story about time travel. That probably won't happen. I've never really understood time travel anyway. Not even when there are ridiculous instruments like flux capacitors involved to bridge the gaps between science and magic.

Maybe The Something Coming is a hooded, gliding ghoul with a scythe and a skeletal claw hanging out the front of his robe. He's the bouncer of this universe, coming to kick me out for breaking one of the rules: "Do Not Get Crushed by Rock" or maybe "Do Not Bleed to Death." People have been kicked out for less.

This could be my eternity: to lie beneath this rock and wait until another girl makes her way down here, so I can plant something shiny like Elizabeth's bridle somewhere deep in

The Woods to lure her over to be crushed. Maybe these whole woods are haunted with crushed girl ghosts and that's what I'm hearing. They're coming to check me out, make sure I'm cool. Which I'm not, so they'll be disappointed.

Perhaps this is how I'm being punished for wandering. Girls can be lost, but they can never purposely wander, and I knew that, learned it from years of caution embedded in everything I saw and read, but I did it anyway. When boys wander alone they grow into men; they learn things about themselves, discover that they're strong and independent. When girls wander alone they're lured by witches to eat poison apples or get caught and ravaged by bandits.

Maybe The Something Coming is Lev, having sensed somehow that his gal was in trouble. He's hunting for me, ready to be my hero, sun and sky and wind ravaging his thin skin as he comes to save me.

And as the gusts of wind wheezed to a halt, the sun comfortable in the sky above me, a simmering afternoon took hold of The Woods. And the world felt small around me. I pumped blood at its center. I am the only *I*. Everything is Easter.

Edrly Our Town

One night after Mr. Ungula had already left, the front door opened. It was Lev. Long-necked Lev. His ears looked bigger. And red. It must be cold outside. His feet beneath his cuffed jeans reminded me of shoes peeking from behind a curtain, someone hiding. I imagined him hiding in our bedroom all those years, watching Julia and me do the things we did in there. Seeing me like that and still thinking I was wonderful. Watching. The still, smiling face of a friendly reptile.

"Hi," he said.
"Hello."
"How's your night?"
"I'm okay."
"Where's your boss?"
"He's out for the night."
"On a date?"
"Probably not."

And he squeezed the fingers of one hand with the other, grouping them tightly together like the stems of a bouquet. He seemed nervous, which made me nervous, so I felt it was best to fill the air with questions.

"Where do you live?" I asked.
"Down the street from here."
"What street?"
"Princess."
"That's not down the street."

And the long-necked Lev laughed and the inside of his mouth was the soft pink of a lizard's.

"I know. I guess I didn't want you to know how far I walk to get here."
"Do you live with both your parents?" I asked.
He nodded. "My dad sells insurance and my mom works at the car dealership. And I go to school."
"Do you have a lot of friends?"
"Not really." He looked down at his feet before he said the next thing: "Can you take me through this place?"
"For free?"
"Yeah, sure. You said your boss isn't around."
"Okay."

In the first room, Early Our Town, I flicked on the light and it shorted. Well, not exactly a short. Sometimes the lights just needed a minute to warm up. Luckily Mr. Ungula kept a flashlight at reception. I used it to illuminate my favorite bits and pieces of the model for Lev. The layers of Early Our Town began with Styrofoam, carefully scalloped to look like cobblestone, topped with a misting of real soot that Mr. Ungula had scraped from his barbeque at home, where I imagined him to cook all kinds of socially unacceptable meats. Maybe that's what always went wrong with his dates. He offered them plates of horsemeat and bulbous grilled Chihuahua eyeballs on kebab sticks.

"Why does it smell like hot dogs in here?"
"Does it?"

I could have just told him that it was the barbeque soot, but I didn't want to make him sick.

"Yeah, it reeks."
"Sorry, this place is a dump."
"No, that's okay, I don't really care about the models anyway."
"Are you sure? There are naked people in Present Day Our Town."
"Easter, I want to kiss you."

And from somewhere deep within the Wonderland, I heard the sound of the bell ringing. The bell on my door, memories buried deep within. It filled my ears until I couldn't really hear, so I stammered, "W-what?" and realized that he'd moved closer.

"I want to kiss you."

And something seemed to take control of my body. And move me closer to the subterranean humanoid, close enough that I could smell the old wet of his skin and see my reflection in his glazed eyes, but not for long because he closed them shut and I closed mine and somehow our lips found each other and his were as damp as I'd imagined them to be, but also very nice in a way, soft and pliant, but maybe I just liked them because my lips had never touched anyone else's before, not because they were the long-necked Lev's lips and were especially gentle and lovely. Then he tried to pry my lips open with his piping hot tongue and I recoiled, scared and unsure of what to do next. I'd wanted to ask Julia to show me how to do it, but she'd ask too many questions. She'd make me do something bad so the long-necked Lev would stop thinking I was wonderful. She'd accuse me of things that weren't true, or maybe they were and I just didn't want to hear them.

"Are you okay?" he asked.

"Yes, I'm okay, I'm just, I have a cold. I'm sick. And I don't want you to get sick."

"That's okay."

"No, really, you're so, delicate and I'm worried that you could catch things from me."

"Delicate?"

"Yeah."

"I wouldn't say I was delicate."

"Well, you're wonderful too, then, and I don't want you to get sick."

He was confused and I couldn't blame him and my heart was beating wildly, off its regular rhythm entirely, moving more like a bell in someone else's hands and less like my heart, and I felt scared and confused and guilty and ashamed, so I told him that Mr. Ungula would be back soon so he'd better leave.

"If I give you my address, can you come over later?"
"I don't know."
"Please?"
"Okay."

He wrote down his address, handed it to me.

"Go around the back, okay?" he said.

And then he opened the door and left me alone in the dark; the flashlight hanging at my side illuminating my feet, the rest of me enveloped in darkness. I felt something in my mouth, something moving the way that Lev's tongue had moved, but this wasn't warm; it was cold and frantic and I reached in and pulled out one of the little bugs that Lev left always behind, that crawled all over him, that likely filled his underground lair. I flicked it away.

Suddenly I heard a loud thump behind me and threw my spotlight on the model, and there, all lit up like a Broadway star, was a very miniature Julia wearing the once-beautiful rags of an aging lady of the night. She began in a puddle of red in the wet street, scabbed with fruit rinds and trash. The red dripped upward into a dress that cinched in the center and oozed up into Julia's bosom, or bazoom. Mr. Ungula always said that bazooms didn't exist anymore. He liked girls to look like toothpaste tubes squeezed in the middle. And that's what Julia looked like. Cinnamon toothpaste.

"Julia, what the hell are you doing here?"
"Cripes, Easter! Can you get that out of my face please?" Her voice boomed though her stature was small.

I flicked off the flashlight and walked toward the light switch that Mr. Harp had put a star-shaped, glow-in-the-dark sticker on so we could find it in the dark. They seemed to be working now.

"Okay, there. Now what the hell are you doing here?"
"No, what the hell is that guy doing here?"

And she kicked one of the Early Our Town figurines: a drunk man who'd nestled himself into the curb for the night. Mr. Ungula had modeled him after a picture of his sister's husband at their wedding reception. Apparently she'd tripped over him in the dark, otherwise I never would have caught her.

With the light on, Early Our Town looked happier. I could see the smiling faces of chimney sweeps, each with a healthy swiping of soot on their rosy cheeks and a ragged broom denting their shoulders. The street became a market of entrepreneurs with their whole families in tow, learning the trade of selling flowers or eggs in the street as well as culti-vating a variety of marketing techniques, such as what the sound of a shrieking child can do for sales or how dressing in rags guarantees higher profits. Men in hats like steam pipes held their noses high, arms hooked with women in warm coats. I had a feeling that Early Our Town looked nothing like this, but I wouldn't dare say that to Mr. Ungula.

"How did you get in there, Julia?" I demanded.

She flung her arms up and screamed a frustrated scream, then turned around and marched into the hotel. The mail slot in the door swung in short, fast bursts after she slammed it, which I'd never seen it do before. Just before it slowed to a complete stop, Julia opened a window in one of the top floor rooms of the hotel and leaned out on her elbows.

"Who's Lev?"

A ball formed in my throat; my heart started flapping again.

"Who?"
"Lev."
"Oh. Just a customer. Nothing special. I wrote his particulars in the book just like the rest of them."

There's that goddamn word again. Particulars. I wanted to excise it from my vocabulary with a scalpel, cut all of its roundness out of my mouth.

"Yeah right."
"Yeah right what?"
"I just saw you kiss him, Easter! I watched you!"
"Goddammit, Julia, why can't you just leave me alone?"

"And you called him wonderful, Easter. You think he's wonderful."

"I said he was a little bit wonderful."

"He called you wonderful, too. I told you that you were wonderful. I told you first. Why do you care so much that he says it?"

"I think you're the most wonderful person in the world, Julia."

"Well you sure don't act like it."

"What do you mean?"

"You want me gone for good. You want to marry a boy and live in a house like ours and be just like The Mother. Fine."

And with that she slipped quickly back through the window, slamming it shut behind her.

"Julia! What are you gonna do?"

But there was no answer.

She wouldn't be back tonight. She'd gone away somewhere I could never know. I locked up and left.

About halfway into heading home I changed my mind and decided to go to Lev's house. I didn't really want to at first. I wanted to just go home, bury my face in my pillow, wait for Julia to creep in next to me, apologize over and over again. But another part of me wanted to taste his lizard mouth again, to have the bells fill my ears and fill my head and fill me up the way that I knew he was supposed to, the way that Amelia's boyfriend did. The way that god, so long ago, had filled me with life and then delivered me to The Mother in peach skin.

I walked all the way to Princess Street and knocked on the back door. After a minute he opened it, smiling wide. We went through his kitchen and into the basement, which was his room. It was cold down there, and damp, and smelled of wet wood and laundry soap. The carpeted floor looked like the multi-colored pebbles of a fish tank, moving somewhat with scribbles of bugs here and there. I sat on the long-necked Lev's bed and he sat next to me, my ears still full of the sound of the bell, so much so that it felt like it was spilling out in the form of hot liquid.

The long-necked Lev sat next to me. He flicked the television on to a quiet, snowy channel so we'd have some light, but not too much. I wished I had my bandana. I wished I could put it over my face.

He told me that he was sixteen. I nodded and said, "That's all right," though I don't really know what that meant. He said, "How come I've never seen you before now?" and I said, "I don't know," and trapped my hands between my thighs, glad that it was so dark down here, underground.

I didn't know exactly what to do next. Amelia had demonstrated through her boyfriend's car window the mating habits of primordial dwarves like her, but not of regular people like me.

And suddenly I felt scared and longed so badly to be in

Julia's arms, to tell her all about tonight, to tell her I only wanted her. But the long-necked Lev had already put my hands in his and was saying something too quietly to be heard over the bell. And before I knew it I was lying down beneath his cold blanket that smelled hairy and dry. And I finally tasted his honeydrop ears, which actually tasted more like raw potato. And he kept kissing me, moving that hot heavy tongue around, not unpleasantly, but I would rather have been lying next to Julia, watching car headlights from outside move through branches and over her sleeping cheek.

We didn't make it through all of the things Amelia had done, and I was happy about that. Later he walked me outside to my bike and when I finally got home there was no Julia in bed for me to whisper my secrets to even though she would probably have plugged her ears and told me she didn't want to hear it anyway.

The hanging

When I woke up the next morning, Julia was home again. She asked me to follow her into the laundry room where she was preparing to hang herself and wanted me to watch. This was a new twist on an old favorite. Julia had hanged before, plenty of times, but it was never a suicide.

She appeared as a witch once, in a book I was reading, and together we wrote a whole hundred pages of us talking while she rode in a wooden jail that had been strapped to a wagon. I pictured her with her feet hanging out through the slats in the back, her ankles brushed with the weeds sticking up from the dirt road, her long dress pulled up and strategically situated to accommodate the unladylike surroundings, her manacled hands kissing wrists and resting on one thigh. Face sooty, but she was happy. That was the first hanging.

Another time she hanged herself accidentally, fetching a long orange extension cord from the garage. It looped down over the rafters, concentrated in brambles on top of them, where it was dark and damp and nasty. She was standing on a stepladder, a wadded section of the cord already in her arms, then reached too far, slipped, and before she knew it an orange loop had grabbed her by the neck and refused to let go. When I found her she was already dead, and I felt bad that she'd been all alone.

I sat with my legs crossed on our laundry room rug while she fixed a hard, unnaturally yellow rope around the metal bar in the closet. A chorus line of men's collared shirts on either side.

"Julia, you don't have to do this."

"I do, Easter."

"You don't!"

"I do. You've made your choice. You want to be like everyone else. You want Lev. And friends. And to be regular. You know that if you stay crazy you probably don't even have to get a job when you grow up? You can just live in a special home with me forever and The Parents will pay for it."

"Yeah."

"But you don't really want that. I can tell."

"I do want it, Julia, but I don't know. I want other things too. Can't I have both of you?"

"No. You'd rather kill me for real."

"No I wouldn't."

"Do you know about hell, Easter?"

And I thought that I did. Hell was living in The Tooth House without Julia. But instead I said, "No."

> "Hell is a library," she said, tightening her fresh knot.
>
> "That really doesn't sound bad, Julia."
>
> "That's because I'm not finished. Hell is a library of books containing every word you've ever said, and videotapes of everything you've ever done."
>
> "So what. Do you have to watch them?"
>
> "No, you don't have to. But would you be able to help yourself? It would be unbearable. I couldn't resist, but I would hate myself after." She gave the noose two good, hard tugs. "Plus, even if you could resist the temptation, you'd eventually get so bored that you'd do anything. And the only thing to read is stuff that you've said and the only thing to do is watch yourself."
>
> "Is there food?"
>
> "I guess, yeah; if you still need food to exist, there can be food."

Julia became exasperated with me easily. She disappeared into the kitchen and I ran my hand backward against the rug, agitating the fibres, attempting to make a pattern. Julia returned to the laundry room with a footstool.

> "Stop that," she said, placing the stool in the closet beneath the noose.

Then she got up onto it.

> "Stop what?" I asked.

"Rubbing the carpet like that. It's gross."

"Who took the videotapes? Who wrote everything down?"

The more I thought about it, the more horrible it seemed.

"I don't know, Easter. It's hell, okay? It was all recorded in some demonic and mysterious way. Cripes."

She put the noose around her neck, tightened it.

"All right, well, I guess that does sound pretty terrible."

"I know, right? I really think that would be the worst possible thing in the world. That's why that's what hell is like."

"Doesn't killing yourself make you go to hell?"

"Oh, Easter, there's no hell. And even if there were, I wouldn't be going there."

"Because you're not real."

"No. Because I'm such a good girl."

Then she kicked the stool out from underneath her feet and let herself hang by her neck from the metal bar. She flailed her arms and got them all wrapped up in the white collared T-shirts, pulling them off their hangers and letting them get tangled up around her wrists. She looked like a bird now, trying to fly with long, white wings, useless, especially in a space as small as a closet.

She kicked her feet around. They searched for the footstool

even if they didn't realize that's what they were doing. I wasn't going to put it back. Julia had made me promise to let her go through with it. And, as usual, she made me promise her that nothing weird was going to happen to her body after she died. As though once she was out of it she still had some right to it. As if there was really a body there at all. Which there wasn't. But Julia was still my sister and I was bound to honor her wishes for that reason. I sat and watched her body until I couldn't keep my eyes open anymore, and when I woke up on the rug the next morning her body was gone and she had put the white shirts back neatly on their hangers.

Two days later I dreamed her funeral. Which I'd never done before. And lying on the ground like this in The Woods made me think of how it must have been for Julia: looking up at the sky, cliffs of dirt on either side, craning over the edge the gloomy, pulled-down faces of all the people who had helped The Mother to change our diapers when we were kids or let us raid their purses for gum or mints so long neglected that the crackle had worn out of the cellophane. Every time someone peeks into a coffin, they always raise that little tissue to their snouts, like they're scared that something is going to fall out. Which is actually quite gross. But really, who best to witness snot falling out of your nose than a dead girl. She's not going to tell anyone. She's not even going to notice. And if she did, she's not really in any place to judge, considering an undertaker has just seen her six ways from Sunday. Cold, naked, unable to resist any position that he decides to put her in.

Or maybe when they raise the tissues to their noses, they're trying to protect themselves from something. Some infection of the dead writhing in the soil, waiting to leap up into an open mouth or flared nostril. If there were any type of ground you were going to catch something from, I guess it would be the cemetery ground, percolating with the volatile exhalations of the recently diseased. Or, in Julia's case, hanged.

It looked like the casket was going to swallow Julia up. Like the maroon satin fabric had once, deceptively, been pulled tight over the open bed of the coffin and when Julia decided to lie down on it she started getting sucked, tightly, into some anonymous hole. Holes are always something to be wary of. In movies, in books, you never hear of someone getting trapped in or falling down a safe, fun, comfortable hole. In fact, holes really get a bad rap when you think about it. I actually quite like holes.

Anyway, there she was: paused, suspended, saved, before she could sink all the way to the bottom. So slow you could barely tell that she was sinking further, frame by frame, fractions of inches, no one could tell but me. I sat between a pair of relatives I'd never met before. Two elderly aunts. Both with long noses that stuck out like tent poles beneath short black veils that obscured their faces but showed their chins and necks. They both sat with their arms knotted around their chests, floral sleeves dampened where a few big fat tear drops had escaped without being noticed, chins doubling, tripling, quadrupling, and dimpled with frowns as they watched Julia's coffin lower into the rectangular hole.

But of course no one is looking at me here under the rock. Except for that thing, maybe, that Something Coming. I closed my eyes and tried to listen for a shuffle or a snapped twig but heard nothing but the leaves.

"Shh!" I said to the leaves, and for a second it seemed as though they might have heard me, might have stopped their twittering for just a scallop of a second. But I still couldn't hear anything. Two squirrels sat on a branch nearby staring at me. One squirrel gave the other a "she's talking to the leaves" look, and even though I'd enjoyed being the only person on earth for a while, turning to wood in The Woods all alone, I suddenly felt very ready for my hero to come and save me soon.

Easter Story

Easter sat at a barstool in the kitchen, her dangling legs making little perpetual motion circles, stirring the air. The Father was crouched in front of her; the breath billowing from his nose warmed her knees. His tongue was out, clipped to his upper lip which was pursed with concentration. He was making X's with his thumbnail into the many oblong mosquito bites she had acquired on her legs that night at the party. He claimed that it was the best way to stop a bite from itching. Easter was dubious. It hurt at first; she begged for calamine, but slowly, the pain began to satisfy the itch; wonderfully, it spread like butter forgotten on the table for a few hours, coating all of the little spots that were driving her insane. The Mother paced the kitchen on the telephone, speaking to the woman whose house they had just left an hour ago, and her voice was beginning to absorb the squealing, anxious quality of their recent host.

"Yes, the bugs were bad tonight, but I think most people made it out of there unscathed."

Pause.

"Well, Easter got a few bites, we're taking care of them."

Pause.

"Thank you for inviting us! We had a lovely evening. We really did. Easter loves to swim, as I'm sure you noticed HA HA HA!"

The Mother had let Easter pick out a red dress for the party and bought her a new bathing suit, pink with pineapples all over it. She fed her cake until she could barely focus and then let her swim five minutes later. She was the only kid there and quickly forgotten as the clouds of bugs thickened and the sky faded to black. She had the whole pool to herself, dark and warmed by an expensive heater. Their host, a woman that The Mother knew somehow, had apologized that the light stopped working in the pool a few days ago.

"I'm sorry, Easter, I hope you're not scared of dark water. Are you brave enough to swim without it?"
"Of course I am," Easter replied from the shallow end.
"And you'll stay in the shallow end, won't you?"
"Yep."

Then the woman turned around and resumed her hosting duties and Easter was left alone for the rest of the evening, which was exactly how she liked it.

Easter performed complicated gymnastics routines, somersaults in the water, spins and dives until she was dizzy and made deaf by the thunderous frenzy of bubbles surrounding her. She tore through the water and the air indiscriminately, splashing and ripping and kicking and flapping. She floated on her belly with goggles on, imagined herself to be drifting through space, slowly, not bound by the perimeters of the pool but one little white and brown and pink-with-pineapples speck in the universe with no destination, no purpose but to float.

And she slipped into the deep end a few times. They didn't notice. She could do anything in here. She considered taking off her bathing suit but was too embarrassed. Someone would definitely notice that: a little naked girl among all of these grown-ups who wore so much stuff.

Easter's legs became riddled with mosquito bites without her really noticing. She'd spent a lot of time sifting through foam noodles and paddleboards in the pool shed, which was rife with pockets of hidden, stagnant water. Dangerous. Now that she was sitting on the barstool in the light of the kitchen, she couldn't believe how many had got her. She thought about how she should really hate bugs more.

The bites went all the way up her legs and she was pretty sure that a small cotton triangle was peeking out from between her thighs beneath the gathered front of her new red dress. She thought that maybe she should adjust it. Or The Father should. Move her dress over her legs to cover it up. But neither of them did. He probably hadn't noticed, but it was all that she could think of. The warm little triangle devoured her thoughts greedily, guzzling them by the clawful, swallowing them whole, smacking its lips for more. The little white triangle. Hide it, Easter. Blood ripened her cheeks. They grew scarlet, like blood moving slowly through a sheet. It's showing, she thought, it's showing, it's showing, it's SHOWING. Her ears rang, full of blood and bell. The Father rose from his knees but kept his head low as though he were bowing to her, his face in Easter's.

> "Is that better?" he asked.
> "Yes." Her heart was beating fast.
> "Are they still itching you?"
> "No."
> "And it didn't hurt that bad, did it?"
> "No."

Easter closed her eyes and felt a hot rush of tears banging against her lids. Why did she have such disgusting things in her head? Why did the little white triangle have to be so greedy for attention?

> "Good," The Father said.

He pulled another barstool over, lifted both of Easter's small ankles up in one hand and placed them softly onto the cool cushion. Then he went downstairs to play the clarinet. "When the Saints Go Marching In" wafted up from the basement and The Mother kept time with her pacing.

hell

With Julia gone, seemingly for good this time, I felt lonelier than ever. I could have been special with her, but I chose to be nothing instead because I'm a fucking idiot.

And without Julia to hate him, Lev seemed somehow less wonderful too. I didn't care if I ever saw him again. He showed up to work smiling. He said "Hello" and moved close to me because after what happened in his underground lair, he must have thought we were boyfriend/girlfriend. I kept my head down the way The Mother does. I didn't look into his frosted eyes.

"What's the matter?" he asked, touching my arm with a cold, slimy hand.

The sound of bells again. Only this time I wanted to shake them out of my ears like warm water after the beach. They felt like intruders, distracting and relentless and loud.

"Nothing."

He smelled so much like skin. Like body hair and saliva all dusted in cheap laundry soap. He was nothing compared to Julia. He was boring and ugly and completely unwonderful.

"I don't think you should keep coming around here," I finally said, after he'd been standing there pretending to peruse the phone books but really upset and dying for me to say something.

"What? Why?"

"Because I don't like you anymore."

Really I couldn't look at him without seeing Julia and feeling so guilty it hurt.

And his eyes welled up with tears and he didn't say anything else, just left and slammed the door, causing a loud groan to lurch through the barrack and Mr. Ungula to emerge from the back: "What on earth was that sound?"

Back at home, I hadn't spoken in days. My stomach hurt. I couldn't eat. The Mother could tell. I could read her concern left to right along the lines of her furrowed brow: she's not eating properly; she looks peaked; she seems tired and withdrawn; why is she slouching like that? We need to fix that hunch, it's so unattractive.

I sunk down further at the dinner table, filled up my spoon with vanilla pudding and hung it vertically from my thumb and my index finger, letting it swing back and forth slowly like a pendulum, globs of it forming a fence around the perimeter of my bowl. I think they thought that vanilla pudding was my favorite. They might even have been trying to cheer me up, but it's hard to tell, as vanilla pudding also happened to be the item in the fridge that required the least amount of effort.

"Honey, what's wrong?" The Mother demanded.

"Nothing."

"It's not nothing. I know it's not nothing. There's something the matter with you and I want you to tell me what it is."

"I'm not going to tell you, all right? So just leave me alone and let me enjoy my pudding for once. You never let me enjoy dessert. Always asking me what's wrong as soon as the good part of the meal comes up."

"What, suddenly you don't like turkey? Why wasn't turkey the good part?"

"I hate turkeys. They're disgusting. All the leftover parts that god didn't know what to do with, that's what turkeys are. Leftovers, leftovers, leftovers."

"Okay, fine. You hate turkeys now."

"And the leftovers."

Then, in an act most unlike her, The Mother cleared her throat loudly and declared:

"You need to get out of this house, Easter. We're going to the lake."

The Father and I both looked at her in shock. Neither of us

had ever heard her declare something so absolutely, make plans without running them by the both of us over and over again, so many times that the entire event was soiled by her incessant nattering about it. We were both too stunned to speak. Which is why we found ourselves that weekend, still dazed by the aftershock of her declaration, squeezing and cramming and folding and bending all of our necessary living utensils into the back of the car like Tetris blocks. Everything smelled like sunscreen. I sat in the back seat waiting for The Parents to finish making sure that anything which could cause a fire or a flood was turned off. The Mother entered stage right, The Father stage left, and Backs of Necks Theatre was about to begin. The scratch and fumble of a microphone switching on and Julia's best impression of a snooty British man filled the back of the car:

"The very handsome Father enters stage left. His wife, The Mother, stage right. Neither will speak for the first little while. One will fumble with the radio while the other makes a mental checklist in his head. If you look closely at the mirror, you can see a pair of eyes checking things off: doors locked, coffee machine unplugged, burners off. Cue the radio. It's something with a reasonably fast beat and while one of them brings the car to growling life, the other begins to move her head to the music. A neck twists like a wet towel, wringing sweat, and she smiles. Off we go."

"Julia! What are you doing here?"

I wanted to grab her, leap into her arms, but strangle her too, kill her for good because she'd made me think it was over. She let me cry and feel terrible and hurt the long-necked Lev.

"What do you mean? This is a family vacation, isn't it?"

"Yeah, but you're dead. You hanged yourself. You made me think you were never coming back."

"Of course I was coming back. When have I ever not come back?"

"You know it was different. You hanged yourself, Julia. And there was a funeral."

"But you're still the same. You got rid of that Lev. I knew you loved me best. Now we'll really shake things up. They'll send us to live somewhere together. We don't ever have to go to The Tooth House again."

"Where will they send us?"

"Maybe to a hospital or a home for extraordinary people. We won't have to go back to school, no jobs, no worries, nothing will matter. Not your ugly face or your imaginary friend."

"Lev didn't think I was ugly."

"I don't think you're ugly either, but you do, so what's the difference?"

"Put on your seat belt."

"Why should I?"

"I don't know. Why do you keep coming back? Why don't you just stay for good, or die for good? Just do one or the other, instead of coming back here all the time and messing me up. That funeral was too much, Julia. You didn't have to do that."

"Well, I had to do something, Easter. I'd never killed myself before. We had to commemorate it somehow."

I covered my ears and squished my eyes shut and whispered something out loud. The Mother twisted her neck back at me, then looked ahead once again.

"You're lucky to have me," said Julia.

"Well I don't feel lucky, Julia. I don't feel lucky at all."

"Think about it, Easter. Anything you don't want to think about, I think about instead. Anything you don't want to do, I do for you. You only deal with the parts of life that you want to. How many people can say that?"

"That's not what it feels like."

"Well, that's what's happening, all right? Now will you get The Parents to change the radio station?"

"You do it. And maybe, whether you're dead or not, I don't want to see you splattered all over the front seat, so put on your goddamn seat belt."

"Fine. And I can't, by the way, ask them to change the channel. And you know that. They never listen to me. Do you want an apple?"

Her hair, as red and alive as ever, slashed her shoulders as she leaned into the cooler to grab the fruit. She handed me an apple.

"Easter, I'm bored. Make up a poem about me."

"Okay. Julia, Julia, Julia. You hanged yourself recently, that must have hurt, the top of your coffin all splattered in dirt. Choosing your funeral dress was a bore, to shop with The Mother is always a chore. There was great debate over in what you would fester, but in the end we went with blue polyester."

"Did you really bury me in polyester?"

"Yep. Now you're going to be hot and itchy for all of eternity."

"You're an asshole."

"I don't care what you think. You're dead."

"Well, you're an awful poet."

It's true. I'm terrible at rhyming. There are a few skills in which kindergarten failed me. I'm also terrible at cutting things out nicely, handling white glue, and napping in the afternoon.

But either way, that was that. Julia and I were in a closed-quarters fight. I had my arms crossed: a warning, a skull-and-crossbones flag on a pirate ship. Leave me alone. Julia didn't look particularly happy either: her eyes were down, chin to her chest. I looked up and let my eyes wind along the nautilus of a sleeping bag. Looked down from there and let my eyes leap from lap to lap. The Mother's fists on her thighs. The Father's hard to see. And a bottle of nail polish remover between Julia's bare knees. And I watched her, comparing the cuticles of her thumbs. Wearing a bathrobe.

A bathrobe; that was odd. Usually when she came back she was wearing what she died in. Which really was polyester this time. That's what you get for hanging yourself and making me watch. A blue polyester one-piece with big purple lapels and a zipper from the knee to the neck.

In an act most unlike her, Julia broke the silence first. Sort of. She resumed Backs of Necks Theatre. Her snooty British voice had seemed to improve over the past hour or two.

"As you can see, a single word has yet to be uttered. But where usually The Mother's neck would be twisting near constantly, an attempt to crack The Father's stony expression with overly make-upped eyes, her neck now remains staunchly forward. And in fact it's his neck that twists every so often, fast so she doesn't notice, but of course she notices. And it's all she can do to stop her heart from beating right out of her chest and flying free and terrified and exhilarated like a bat once trapped in a room. You'll notice how deliberately she's dressed this morning. Her chest pushed up to her throat, a necklace buried between the hills. Still they don't speak. But for the first time in family vacation history, The Father's expression seems to have splintered ever so slightly. Has The Mother worn him down with her patheticness? Or is something more sinister afoot?"

I interrupted her: "Julia? How did it get this way?"

She furrowed her brow at me and bundled her robe up closer to her chin.

"It got this way because he hates her, Easter. And he hates you, too."

"Then why does he stay?"

"Because he's lazy. And mean."

Outside the Lake

The lake was always the temperature of inadequately micro-waved mashed potatoes. It was as still as mashed potatoes, too. To dip one foot into the lake was to have it absorbed, sucked up, devoured. To kick that foot would be to gouge the surface. But you would never do that. Because the lake was like a large, sleeping thing, a lazy, deeply breathing beast that it wasn't wise to disrupt. And you knew that. When you swam in it, which was rarely, you stepped in gingerly, letting the wet, furry bottom of the lake sniff at you, evaluate you, lick you clean. Then, once it was sure you weren't up to any-thing, it let you move.

Boats glided hesitantly here. Paddles dipped slowly into the water: wooden spoons spreading icing on a too-warm cake.

There's long, dry grass growing all along the perimeter, and when the wind moved through it the sound of agitated rattlesnakes filled the air. But don't worry because it's just the sound. No real rattlesnakes hiding in the grass. In fact,

Hector was the only other living thing that I had ever seen around here. But that might be because he was so good at his job, which I'll get to.

On this lake was the cabin that my family and I had been renting sporadically since I was little. Hector was the name of the dog who lived there. He was black with skin that hung from his face like unfolded sheets and red pooled around his eyes. He was a friendly dog and would let you tangle your fingers in his skin for a while, but he had a job and that job was to kill little rodents that hung around and pestered the renters. Like squirrels. He liked me, so sometimes he would bring me his victims, but I wasn't allowed to scold him because his employers asked me not to. So I accepted these gifts graciously, patted his head, then sent a stick flying into the water for him to fetch because I couldn't stand the sight of him gloating over a kill.

On windy nights I would sit in the long grass, pulling out handfuls like clumps of hair and holding them up in the air to let the wind take them away. Hector would always find me and let me warm my hands on his belly, then curl up halfway behind me, still open like a dried millipede. That way I could snuggle my way into him, between his paws, lean back against his belly.

Other times I would row a little boat out to the middle of the black lake, careful not to disturb it too much, and hold a fishing rod out for a while. I never caught anything. I'm pretty convinced that there was nothing alive in that lake either. Not a single fish or eel or plankton or mussel or bug. So when I was skewering worms onto a hook I was sending them into a vast, threatless nothing. A cruel, purposeless mission into the abyss for my entertainment. Maybe I made these worms appreciate life more when I was done. I might be god to them. And I liked skewering them. Pulling one by its end out of the bucket, watching him writhe a bit. Long, alive, engorged. Then I would stick him one. Penetrate his segments with a sharp end and watch white stuff come out. But he was still alive. He was always alive. Writhing around still, wrapping himself around the metal barb. Hector would watch me from the shore sometimes barking at random moments just to startle me.

"Shut up, Hector!" I'd scream just as loud. "You're scaring the fish away!"

And we'd both chuckle over that one because we knew that there weren't any fish to scare anyway.

Inside the Lake

Julia and I slept in the giant attic that skulked above the other rooms in the cabin. We shared a small bed in which neither of us slept very comfortably, each with half our limbs falling over the side and settling into some crooked, almost comfortable position. Julia was always awake before me, into her bathing suit and strolling along the beach before the sun was out to warm everything up. She said that she liked to have her goose bumps rubbed off by the sun, but really it was that she didn't like Hector very much and he didn't like her either, so she disappeared.

When I woke up alone this morning it was to the shrill reverberations of The Mother telling The Father what to do. Which I'd never heard before. In fact, at first I wasn't sure if it was The Mother's voice at all. I sat up in bed on my knees and peeked through the window. My fingers gripped the headboard and I moved my lips against my tight knuckles.

The Mother was standing in the yard, which was mapped with giant masses of dead grass. Brown and balding like the irregular pattern of hair that grows on an old man's back. Her bare feet were on this old man's shoulders, her ankles slim and imprisoned by the long frays that hung from her shortened white jeans like crystal teardrops from a chandelier. The jeans were hoisted high over her tilted-sideways waist, on which she'd placed one red-fingernailed hand. Her midriff was bare and still medium rare, having only spent a few hours in the sun so far. Cheap boning made its way up her rib cage; the skeleton of her floral tank top. Little cups were provided to hold the boobs. Boob cups. And hers had settled there like a thick liquid. She might have even been able to pour them into martini glasses for dinner later. Her sunglasses were white and thick and plastic and her lips were red. She was clucking directions at The Father as they attempted to install a croquet court together.

He stood tall with a mallet over his shoulder and a bag of wickets hanging from the fingers of his other hand. On his big feet black sneakers, bare legs to the thigh, then a pair of khaki-colored shorts, a red sweater encasing the inklings of a gut, dark sunglasses on his pale face. He was looking at The Mother impatiently, probably wondering what the hell had gotten into her. In that voice that didn't sound at all like hers, she was telling him where to stick the wickets.

"One: use your mallet to drive a stake directly into the center of the court."

A clanging clonk.

"All right, done."

"Now, place the next wicket twenty-one feet from—"

"Why are we putting a croquet court here? There's no grass. There hasn't been any grass for years. A proper croquet court is meant to have grass."

"I don't care if it's not the exact same croquet court that the Queen of England has. I want a croquet court, so please keep going."

"I just think that it's incredibly stupid to put in an improper court."

"Just pay attention. Please. Twenty-one feet from the center. Scoot."

Scoot.

And he did. The Father scooted his way across the court, his posture sulking, his face puzzled, trying to recall the point at which he scooted when she said so.

He readied the first wicket to smash in. I had to stop watching because I kept picturing the ground as that old man's back and couldn't stand the sight of The Father ramming metal hoops into it. I decided not to go outside until they were done. Instead I just listened to them banging.

The Mother telling The Father what to do was something I hadn't seen in a very long time, possibly ever. Usually she did whatever he told her to do, or she predicted his needs first so he didn't even have to tell her and he could just keep being a big, silent mystery. And the more she resembled a doormat, the more he seemed to treat her like one. Her willingness to bend over backward to accommodate; her messy, gushing, wide-open, over-the-top love for her family: these things were all incredibly irritating. And it made you want to abuse her for it. See how far you could push her before she snapped. It made me wonder if The Father wasn't always a big black mystery, making noises from the basement, grunting replies, ignoring everyone. Maybe she made him that way. And she made me the way that I was, too. She taught me to worship him unconditionally. To wear it all over my face like raw egg, to let him treat me however he wanted, to let him push it as far as he wanted because I would always want him.

But it seemed she had a new strategy, a strategy that appeared to be working. She would be mean to him, look less like a doormat, squawk orders at him in tight clothes so that he didn't know what to do but obey. Now he might love her again, and want her, and I would be the only pathetic one left in The House.

I couldn't think about it anymore without wanting to scream. So I decided that I would distract myself with breakfast. Then I might choose a movie to watch. The cabin came equipped with three: an old horror movie called *Freaks*, the cartoon version of *Robin Hood*, and finally, someone's colonoscopy, probably the man who owned the cabin, maybe he got off on dropping videos of his colon into houses with children in them. Either way, I wouldn't make the mistake of watching it a third time.

Breakfast was a bowl of Rice Krispies with chocolate chips on top and a tall glass of tomato juice, which I consumed while leaning over the local newspaper. A squirrel had reunited a man and his son this past weekend. And a quadriplegic won the lottery. Scratch tickets. I wondered if she was going to give a portion of the money to the person who scratched the ticket for her. I also wondered what percentage of her clothing had Winnie-the-Pooh characters on it. I'll bet it's a big portion. Every time you see an adult with Piglet on their shirt you can bet that they're buying or have already bought some scratch tickets. Sometimes The Mother buys scratch tickets too, and once when I was with her with at a convenience store I asked her why.

> "Mom. You're never going to win. Ever. You're basically just paying to be disappointed." I'd heard The Father say this to her as well.
> "I know, Easter," she said, fingering through her wallet for her credit card, "but you've got to put yourself out there sometimes."

Her eyes were carefully scanning the tray of tickets that lay before her. I wondered what she could be looking for, how one ticket could be differentiated from another. I also wondered how buying a lottery ticket could be considered "putting yourself out there." So I asked her.

"I don't know what you mean by that," I said. "How are you putting yourself out there? You're not doing anything but choosing a ticket."

But she was too busy trying to get the storekeeper's attention to explain.

Another clang from outside. Wickets were being planted and a deformed croquet court was born. I covered my ears. The Mother walked in, loud heavy steps replacing her regular quiet way of walking.

"Good morning, honey."

She ran a hand along my hair before heading toward the sink. I shook it away like I always do.

"Morning," I replied with my mouth full.

"Do you smell something?" she asked me, using the inside of her forearm to dab the glow from her forehead.

"No."

"Ugh, really? Something smells awful in here, Easter. What did you do?"

"Are you seriously asking me that? What do you think I did? I took a giant crap in the corner, Mom. Was that wrong?"

The Mother laughed and shook her head and pulled two glasses from the cupboard and filled them with water.

"What's the matter with you today?" I asked.

"What are you talking about?"

"You're different. There's something strange about you."

"I don't know what you're talking about, Easter." She was lying.

"You do know. You're acting like someone else."

"And who exactly am I acting like?"

I looked outside in the direction of The Father. She stood there waiting for an answer. I looked back down at the newspaper, and she sighed and left the room.

I did smell something, though. Something awful. I got up and stood in the middle of the living room, gathering my brow into a wrinkled mass, eye squeezed shut, lips pursed tight, trying to concentrate on where the smell was coming from. But there were no leads. Just the enormously stagnant grip of the smell itself.

I searched. Starting with the undersides of things, sliding my hands beneath every couch, chair, dresser, end table, collecting mittens of dust bunnies and shoe leavings. That's what The Mother called the stuff that blusters in with you from outside when you walk through the door.

I lifted cushions and moved furniture and unloaded shelves and drawers and cabinets. The smell never intensified regardless of what I pulled up or knocked over or unearthed; not a single clue. It was an unsolvable puzzle. I wanted it to resemble anything at all, to get heavier, to reek from one direction, to emanate the stink like a signal tower: beep, beep, beep. I stood up straight, still, tall. I made myself totally available to the stink, open to it for signs. I listened closely. Beep, beep, beep. I tore through baskets of magazines and crossword puzzle books and stray crayons, I pulled off the cushions on the couch and dragged my fingers between all the cracks. BEEP, BEEP, BEEP. I tore through closets, fisted boots and hats and other seasonal closet clothing to make sure they were empty. BEEP BEEEP BEEEEP. I stood swaying before the gutted closet, trying to spontaneously generate or pry from myself some new sense capable of locating this smell. A smell has got to make itself known in more ways than just the nose! I tore the doors off the kitchen cupboards, yanked up floorboards, pierced the softness beneath my nails on flimsy vinyl bathroom tiles. BEEEP BEEEEP BEEEEEP. I ripped up the carpet, turned every table upside down, pushed the TV over. BEEEEP BEEEEEP BEEEEEEP. Such a squealing smell! But I couldn't find anything anywhere.

That night over dinner The Mother expressed her repulsion about the smell while we were all trying to eat chicken pot pie together, on bar stools around the kitchen island. Everyone's knees off to one side awkwardly. The dining room table was covered in a giant croquet blueprint that The Mother was making a decorative project of to put up in our real house. She was getting what she wanted left, right, and center. Last year The Father never would have tolerated us eating at the kitchen island because The Mother had a giant art project on the table, but this year, in her boob cup shirts and in her new way of talking to him, she was getting everything.

"Good god, what is that smell? Does anyone else smell that?"

"No," I said.

I wanted to be the one to find whatever it was that smelled, so I couldn't have her snooping around.

"Really? You don't smell that."

She looked at me as though she couldn't possibly believe that I couldn't detect the near-unbearable stench that was slapping all of us in the face right now.

"Nope."

"If that's true, then there's something wrong with your nose. We need to get your nose checked." She turned to The Father. "Can you believe this? Do bad noses run in your family? Easter can't smell that awful smell."

He walked over and put a hand on my forehead.

"She feels fine to me."

She looked at him in that antagonistic, stunned way that he hated. Perhaps he was on to her manipulation, had been on to her the whole time, and right now, all of a sudden, he might lunge at her over the kitchen island, grab her throat and squeeze. He might do it with one hand and then use the other to scoop steaming hot chicken pot pie from the disposable tray into her face, smear it up her nose, into her eyes. I might walk over with the salt and shake some on her. Then

The Father and I would get into the car and go back home together. When I found it, I'd show him my secret smell.

He didn't, though.

All he said was "I was joking," and he poured a spoonful of pot pie onto his plate.

"We should really call Gary about this. Can you stand this smell?"

He shook his head slowly, not really listening to her, just agreeing.

"All right, then, it's settled. I'm calling Gary tomorrow."

Gary was the guy who owned the cabin and rented it out to people like us. I bet it really was his colon in the video. He looked like the type to have digestive problems; his bottom lip always a stiff half circle, one big paw at the base of his distended belly, a faded golf shirt aching to stay tucked into his pants over it. A bald head, ruddy cheeks, and an unhealthy colon from what I could tell.

The Mother liked to make a big deal of everything. Who cares if the place smelled like diarrhea? She always had to meddle.

I wanted to twist the end of her nose off and chew on it like bubble gum. But I didn't.

Instead I waited until they both went to bed, waited until the air was so quiet that not even the ghost of the hammering croquet mallet lingered. Then I began another exhaustive search, made more difficult this time because I had to be careful not to wake The Parents. I rifled through drawers, unloaded shelves, peeked under the cracks of locked doors. Nothing at all.

And the next morning I woke up early to search again, just in time to see Julia's sandaled foot passing over the mat in front of the door, the corner of her beach towel flicking up like a super hero's cape.

"See ya," I whispered uselessly.

She wasn't one for goodbyes.

Easter Story

Easter sat behind the screen door watching the ground bloat with rain. She wasn't the type of girl to be bothered by rain. In fact, she hated when nice days made her feel guilty about just wanting to stay inside. Little droplets clung to the wire screen, wild with the knowledge of being temporary. The sky was the suffocated white of bright sun fighting through clouds and as the door beaded more heavily with drops, a cross-stitch shadow began to appear on Easter's face.

The image shivered to life: a night at dinner, Easter's head on The Mother's lap, a candle about to make a smoldering exit via the ominously ebbing pool of wax surrounding it. An elbow is twitching, tickling Easter's ear. This must have been what woke her up. The elbow becomes a bangled arm becomes a slight wrist, a hand unsteadily gripping a long stemmed glass. It belonged to The Mother. They were both occupying the wide wicker loveseat that sat on the deck all summer and moved to the table when they barbequed.

217

The air was unfamiliar. Belonging to an hour that Easter rarely saw. Four in the morning, perhaps? An alien crispness. An impossible color. The Mother had been sitting there all night. Easter must have at some point made the barely conscious decision to stay up with her. The half-eaten casserole spoiled in the center of the table and three plates were set.

Easter was six years old and could still curl up comfortably on one cushion of a loveseat like a cat. She didn't want The Mother to know that she was awake. There was something secret about this moment. So she pretended that her ear had never been tickled by that slender, unsteady elbow.

The Mother was mumbling something. Her lips moving so slowly, so slightly, moving barely more than the raindrops shivering in the wire screen. The Lonely made her ugly and beautiful at once.

And of course you couldn't really tell all of that from the waterdrop cross-stitch picture in the screen door. From the quivering picture in the screen door it just looked like a mother and a kid on a deck in the summer, no tickled ears or coagulated casserole or whispered mumblings to someone or no one. Then the raindrops, weak and exhausted from their time embedded in the wire, trickled to their deaths.

Easter thought about the way that pictures often failed her, incapable of telling a story in full, always missing the most important parts of a moment.

She remembered a picture she found in Phyllis the Fucking Bitch's basement. She'd brought it upstairs to examine over toast with jam. *Three brothers in bathing suits, the tallest one holding a spewing hose proudly, each with wide grins on their young faces and wet, spiky hair. The picture was protected by a brown frame. Phyllis the Fucking Bitch's reflection appeared in the glass and Easter's lips parted slightly.*

> *"Those are my cousin's boys," Phyllis said.*
> *"Oh," Easter replied.*
> *"Would you believe that they were all born without tongues?"*

Easter's face dropped in shock. She furrowed her brow, trying to find some clue in the picture, but there was none. All of these boys born without tongues and you would never know. Easter shivered and Phyllis the Fucking Bitch's reflection disappeared.

The Smell

I decided that I needed to enlist some help if I was going to find what was causing The Smell. So I went outside to find Hector.

He was broiling in the sun, the air rippling off his warm black body. He lay on his back, the skin on his jowly face pooled around his upside-down skull, revealing his enormous teeth in a friendly way. I stepped into his sunlight, casting a tall shadow across his face. He looked up at me.

"Wanna come inside and help me find something?"

He rolled over lazily, shook the sleep from his head, and trotted behind me toward the cabin. He'd know what he was looking for as soon as he walked in.

He took a big sniff and went straight for the fancy dish cupboard, digging his way through, crashing teacups and small, useless dishes, burying his face in a large silver serving dish.

After a few seconds he pulled something out and dropped it gingerly to the floor, leaving behind dollops of froth from the corners of his mouth.

A squirrel. Dead. Its small, round belly bloated with gas, eyes open and dry like little black beetles. His nose was pink, his fur all gray. With my hands overlapped on my mouth and nose, my eyes began to expand with tears. A squirrel tail without life is the saddest thing you could ever see. Without that vivacious electric eel inside, controlling the fluff, squirrel tails just looked like a sad pile of dust bunnies. And that was what I'd mistaken it for when I'd dug around in that cupboard.

"Thanks, Hector!" I warbled, not meaning it. "You're a good boy," and I rubbed his neck.

Suddenly a tiny squeak severed his praise. This squirrel was alive! But just barely. Unfortunately, Hector was all business. As soon as he realized that the little thing was breathing, he scooped it up and crushed it in his big powerful jaws. A fast, merciful death, but still a gruesome one. He dropped the punctured thing at my feet, trotted back outside, and worked his way back into the spot where the grass was bent and imprinted with his once-sleeping shape to resume his nap.

I scooped up the lifeless bundle, laid it in a shoebox, wrapped the shoebox tight in electrical tape, and stuffed it in a bundle of hopefully odor-suppressing blankets in mine and Julia's attic room.

The Incident

I debated showing Julia the squirrel. When you take that kind of step in your life, becoming a person who hides dead animals in their room, it's kind of hard to come out about it. It's like telling your family you're a drug addict or something. People aren't going to take it very well, and it's not the most flattering thing in the world to be. So I waited.

I sat the whole day and night with the shoebox I'd put it in, watching, wondering if there was still a squirrel in there at all, wanting to unwrap it but scared. On the bed, with my legs crossed and the shoebox in my lap, I read a fairy tale from the big, stately Hans Christian Anderson book we kept up there. A story about a poor girl, little and cold and selling matches in the street. It was very late when Julia finally came home.

"You're still awake," she said when she entered.

She spoke these words in such a way that I had absolutely no idea how she meant them. *You're* still awake: disappointed.

You're still a*wake*: happy. You're *still* awake: impressed. But being awake isn't that impressive. Unless you'd been in a coma. I nodded because it seemed the best way to respond to something that you didn't really understand anyway. It was my usual response when hobos with no teeth or people with impossibly thick accents tried to communicate with me. Nod, nod, nod.

"What've you got on the bed there?" she asked, noticing my shoebox.

"I'll show you, but you have to promise not to freak out."

"Oh god, Easter, what is it?"

I lifted the lid off the shoebox.

"What part of that was supposed to freak me out?"

It was empty. I was shocked. It had been there. I'd picked it up and placed it inside. I'd seen the small hole where Hector's tooth pierced his inflated little belly. Where had it gone? I looked around, scared. Hadn't I been watching the whole time? I peed once, for two minutes tops.

"I had a squirrel in here," I finally said.

Julia looked alarmed. "Is it inside the house some-where?"

"No, it was dead."

"Gross, man. What's wrong with you?"

"Nothing's wrong with me! There was this terrible smell, Julia, couldn't you smell it? Strong enough to make you gag. It was making The Mother insane. I looked everywhere and couldn't find it so I finally got Hector to help me and he found it, Julia! But it wasn't dead yet, it was just barely alive, but Hector could tell and you know what he's like, as soon as he heard it squeak he killed it."

Then I had to concentrate for a moment not to cry.

"So you decided to peel the stinking dead squirrel off the floor and bring it into our room to show me?"
"Yeah!"
"You're insane. This is what happens when you spend too much time with that stupid dog."
"I am *not*, Julia! I am not insane. I'm telling you, this squirrel was in the cupboard, he was in that big serving dish."

Her eyebrows quivered, her mouth cracking at the corners. She was about to laugh.

"Goddammit, Julia, you put it there, didn't you! No wonder it's gone."

She burst out laughing, so hard she could barely contain herself. She laughed herself backward, plopping onto a beanbag chair on the floor where she finally exhaled herself back into a normal state. Her legs made triangles with the floor.

"Why would you do that, Julia? Why would you make me think I was going crazy? Why are you such a terror?"

"Me? You've been so boring I can barely stand to look at you!"

"What else do you want from me? I picked you! I want you! Why are you still being so mean?"

"Maybe you did some serious damage, Easter. Maybe you hurt my feelings too much this time."

I stared at her in the way that forces people to explain themselves further. So that's what Julia did.

"You think if you're normal, he'll like you more. You think if you bring a boy home he might even be jealous, or at least feel protective of you. But he won't, Easter. I'm the only family you've got. Why can't you see that?"

I felt guilty. Incapable of denying it because it was true. I'd been having fantasies of life without her, life without The Mother too. A house with just me and The Father, where he'd have to pay attention to me and he'd want to because I'd be my better self.

I kept quiet because I knew that if I tried to lie, she'd know. So she painted her face all smug, got up, shut off the light, and snuck under the covers on her side of the bed.

Besides the shoebox and the too-small bed, there were a few other things in our attic room. There was a desk with two drawers both filled with broken pencils and crayon nubs and crinkled pieces of paper of varying degrees of usefulness. There was a bookcase where our Hans Christian Anderson book lived, as well as lots of others that Julia and I would read from out loud on nights when it was too hot to sleep. There was a white nightstand with a lamp on it and a floral sheet dividing our room from a storage area filled with tent poles and camping stoves and inflatable mattresses. A large box of matches peeked from beneath the sheet like a shoe. I thought of Lev's feet peeking beneath the cuffs of his jeans and I wished he were hiding behind the curtain, somehow able to see that I didn't want to be mean to him. That I had to be. Because I already had a Julia and there wasn't room for two people who thought I was wonderful.

In the middle of the night, after our fight, I heard Julia rustling behind it, her back end sticking out in front.

> "Hey!" I hissed. "What are you doing back there?"
> "What?" I'd startled her. She shot up like a splash and the sheet moved like a disturbed pond behind her. "What? Oh, nothing. Just go back to bed."
> "Ha! Yeah right. What've you got behind your back?"
> "What? Nothing."

I swung my legs out of bed and marched as authoritatively as I could over to her without making too much noise. This would have been a terrible time to wake The Parents.

> "Julia, for god's sake, I know it's not nothing. Just show me what you've got. You know you can't do this. It's not fair."
> "Oh my god Easter, fine. You're such a brat."

With that she slammed the big box of matches down into my hand with a thunderous rattle.

"What are you doing with these?"

"Nothing."

"You're full of 'nothings' tonight."

"Well, I don't know, Easter. I just wanted to play with them a little bit."

"In the middle of the night?"

"What's fun about playing with matches during the day?"

"I guess that's true."

I sat down on the floor gently and spread my nightgown over my crossed legs, letting my knees provide the support beams for a little hammock. I then dumped a healthy number of matches on top. Julia sat down across from me and made her own nightgown match-dish. Hers was bigger than mine so she poured in even more matches. We smiled at each other. Julia always had the best ideas. I wasn't mad at her anymore about the squirrel.

"I'm not mad at you anymore, Julia."

"I'm not mad at you either."

"I love you and I want to keep you forever."

She smiled and lit the first match and it came to life aggressively. Strong and high and bright but out too soon. Only the shortest bit of limp, withered head drooped from the end of the stick.

"Damn," Julia whispered. She tossed it.

She tried another and produced the same overly enthusiastic result. Again the dud was tossed. Again and again. Soon there were dozens of singed sticks piling up around us like a campfire.

"Mom and Dad are going to smell this, you know. They're going to think we're setting the cabin on fire."

She lit another match and we both watched with held breath as it slowly quivered to life. A little creature finally awakened. Our new pet. Delicate. Proverbially pink and unspoiled as a baby. But not for long. Its dark center lub-dubbed with heat. It throbbed in our ears. And somewhere in its deepest, hottest core, a picture came to life: a pair of legs over a jeaned lap, sunlight streaming in and emblazoning the downy hair misted all over the young, lazy legs that were now squirming somewhat. Toes thuddling. Slowly a hand, fingernails the size of quarters, came down on her tennis-ball knees and the match went out.

"Did you see that?" I asked.
"Of course I saw it. I did it."

She lit another match.

The flame came to a jagged end and danced like a chorus line of bright little toes. They were lapped at over and over again by the heat coming up from the center of the match. But in a second that center became a long pink tongue, devouring the tiny toes one by one from the end of a pudgy foot. Wrapping around and sucking down like plucked grapes. But the foot didn't bleed. It just kept producing little toes to be inhaled. A broad smile, a mouthful of toes. Toe teeth. Then the match went out.

"Let me do one."

So she handed me the box of matches. Her teeth glistened in the dark room.

I lit the match. And wondered what would happen if I were to kill Julia myself. Hold this match under the hem of her dress, watch it erupt, watch her spin around like a firecracker, skin melting, flesh dropping, charred flops splattering on the floor.

The Fire erupted in red, a dark sore in the center, moving out into a frenzied shell of orange. It was being prodded, poked, by some undetectable but furious wind. Rubbed and irritated, stoked. Then it hollowed out through the middle and became our tub, filled with water, glowing red and almost perfectly still. Floating in the middle of the water was a small gray squirrel, drowned and bloated, eyes as still as little black bugs. The squirrel became the head of the match which began unfolding from the inside out, getting bigger and bigger and I realized that I was holding a handful of matches, blazing.

The flame got bigger and hotter and then I was in an entirely different room. A white room with neon green lines like hills and valleys waltzing over the walls. Blue and red polka-dots puncturing the scene. I smelled clean laundry and rubbing alcohol and I felt hands all over my body, lifting things, poking things, pressing things, moving things, holding things, turning things, bending things, flicking things. Some of these hands even had special devices; pulling things, tapping things, probing things, stinging things. I felt like I was getting a makeover. I was going to get up from this bed that I was lying on, walk to the mirror and see a whole new face staring back at me.

I realized later that I was in a hospital.

I remembered Julia saying, "Easter, no! No! NO!"

And she'd been on fire, flinging bright bits of her nightgown through the air as she spun, each bright bit a fiery bird flying frantically and colliding with everything. The sheet that divided our room from the camping gear, the sheet from which the matches peeked at us in the first place. It went up quickly, shards of it joining the flock and soaring to our bed and our pile of books. Everything prickled; my eyes burned. We must have baked like Salty the cat in his trash can tomb before it woke The Parents and they called the fire department.

Recovery

I've never been able to remember the first second that I wake up. It's like this one tiny event that happens every day that I'm physically incapable of being aware of. Maybe it's because the brain doesn't work enough at that point to start holding on to things. So even though you wake up, you don't actually realize it because you have no idea what it's like. Maybe it's horribly painful. A feeling like your eyes have been soldered shut in the night and then sliced open like a paper cut in the morning, but because you don't remember it, it may as well have never happened. But I don't like the idea of waking up and not realizing it. I want it to be exactly how I imagine it to be.

When I woke up in the hospital, I knew I was awake before I even opened my eyes. It was very strange waking up in the world behind your eyelids, pulled from the depths of your subconscious into the dark.

I think it must have been the unnatural position that the

doctors put me in to sleep. Flat on my back with my head elevated slightly and crammed between two pillows, my arms along my sides, my hands in fists around wads of sheet. I was unnaturally straight and everything in my body was very aware of it having been placed that way.

I opened my eyes as slightly as I could and spotted The Parents in low chairs upholstered in a raw-looking, rose-colored fabric. They each had a Styrofoam cup placed on a wooden armrest and were looking up at a man in a white coat who had his rounded back to me. He sat on a black leather stool with three wheels and I noticed that he was moving, slowly and ever so slightly, over a groove in between tiles on the floor. Slowly, slightly, thump. Slowly, slightly, thump. Back and forth and back and forth. Slowly, slightly, thump. Maybe he was performing some kind of subliminal humping routine, an old doctor trick that makes bad news go over better because the sick or bereaved are brewing a reaction to this undercurrent of unsolicited lechery, a distraction from the tragedy.

Probably not. Probably he just did it because that's what he did when he was sitting on a chair with wheels. He probably did it in his office too, in his desk chair, and at home in front of the computer at night. I'll bet that when he sat on a couch or in a dentist's chair he went crazy after a little while, longing desperately for the slowly slightly thump, slowly slightly thump satisfaction that he got from these other chairs in his life.

My whole body had the feeling somewhat of being suspended, or perhaps it was the feeling of being all together too warm and prickly. Whatever I was wearing didn't feel like my clothes. It felt like a hospital gown, which meant that someone in this hospital had to change me, force my lifeless limbs into the arm holes and tie up the back. Someone around here had seen me naked and I had no idea how to avoid them. This was torturous.

I moved my eyes to the left (no Julia) and to the right (no Julia). Perhaps she was gone for good this time. This time I could phone the long-necked Lev and tell him I'm sorry. That I wanna hear bells with him and be normal forever. And then I felt so guilty that I ached. Guilty that I hadn't been there to take care of Julia's body and guilty because even though I loved her more than anything, I really hoped she wouldn't be back. But I couldn't move or cry or let on that I was awake because I was trying to listen to what the doctor was saying. He spoke quietly with his back turned to me. He said something about The Fire, that it's what happens when a young girl is very lonely and looking for attention, and he thought it would be best to separate me from them for a while. The Mother growled something about abandonment and The Father said something about how no one had even said the word "abandon." I couldn't really understand any of it.

Before I could further eavesdrop, The Mother caught sight of wetness between my eyelids.

"Easter? Easter, honey, you're awake."

It sounded more like the command of a hypnotist. I opened

my eyes as fully as I could and pictured them swirling under her control. They asked me how I felt, did I remember what had happened, could I hear them? Fine, sort of, yes, I answered. Then came the assault: what the hell is the matter with you, you could have killed yourself, what possessed you to do such a thing? I don't know, I know, I don't know. Sorry.

"Sorry!" The Mother shrieked. "Easter, for god's sake, you could have killed all of us! Do you realize that? What were you thinking?"

"I don't know."

The doctor interjected, whispered something in The Mother's ear.

She cleared her throat and continued:

"Well, we're going to have to get to the bottom of this, Easter. You can't just go around setting our homes on fire."

She looked at The Father to see if he wanted to say anything. His eyes were on my hands, which I was using to squeeze little hills into the sheets and then flatten them out. The Mother realized that he had no intention of addressing me, so covered up quickly.

"We love you very much, honey, and we're just so worried about you."

Then she combusted spontaneously into sobs.

I should have told them that it was what they'd always wanted. Julia was gone and I was normal so now The Father could love me and The Mother could drop dead and everything would be perfect.

I recalled the first and only time I attempted to give credit where credit was due: a horrible idea of Julia's to unscrew the tops of our iron bedposts and pour water inside to make a waterbed. They filled and leaked and seeped into the floorboards, making four giant stains on the ceiling below, brown with irregular edges like continents on a map. The Mother sat me down on the steps, asked me why I did it.

> I said, "It wasn't me, Mom, it was Julia. It was her idea. All I did was get the water."
>
> "Easter, would you please stop with that stuff? I can't exactly tell your dad that *no one* did this, that it just appeared on the ceiling. You did this. Just tell me that *you* did this."
>
> "But I didn't!"
>
> "You did, Easter! Stop lying!"
>
> "I'm not lying!"

That night, Julia and I listened through the floor. The Parents fought about the watermarks, about my lying. And Julia, after refusing to speak to me for an hour and a half, finally broke the silence.

> "I can't believe you told them it was me."
>
> "It was you."
>
> "Easter, you're such an idiot. It was you. You did it."
>
> "I did not! You told me that we could make a waterbed! It was your idea! You filled the posts yourself!"

"Easter, don't you get it? It was you. *You.* You're the one who does things. If you tell them about me again, I'll kill myself for real. I'll never come back and you'll be all alone here. Is that what you want?"

"No."

"I didn't think so."

Then the memory evaporated, burst by an angry-looking Phyllis opening my hospital-room door.

She wore a long linen dress, coral, with gold chains around her neck and wrists. It reminded me that it was summertime outside, even though it was cold in here. The Mother and The Father looked up, The Mother shocked, her eyes and mouth round. She sucked back up her sobs and stood up, then sat back down again, mumbling something to herself. Somehow Dr. Slowly Slightly Thump knew to get up and leave. He nodded at me before he did. The Mother stood up again. Phyllis hadn't looked at me yet.

"Why didn't you call me?" Phyllis said quietly through clenched teeth.

"I just—I didn't think of it. What are you doing here?" replied The Mother.

"Do you have any idea how embarrassing it is not to know that your own granddaughter is in the hospital?"

The Mother just looked down at her feet. The Father pulled his foot over his knee, rested his head on the back of the chair, and rolled his eyes back as far as they could go so he could glimpse the section of room next to me. Just like mine, curtain pulled back. I bet he was noticing how tight the sheets were. Pulled perfectly snug over the beds. Like Saran Wrap over a bowl, so tight as to be invisible. A thing of beauty. I'd noticed it too, I wanted to tell him that we liked the same things, but I couldn't say anything at all.

"Never mind the fact," Phyllis continued, "that you told that *woman* she set the cabin on fire."

That caused The Father to lift his head, return to the conversation with a furrowed look at The Mother.

"Who did you tell?" he asked.

The Mother expanded with tears once again, exploding with explanation.

"Well, I had to call Gail!" (that was Amelia's mother). "She was collecting the mail and watering the flowers so I had to tell her that we'd be longer than we planned. And I don't know, she asked me how the … the trip was going and I couldn't hold it in."

The Father dropped his head into his open palm, ran his fingers through his hair. Then he got up.

"Anyone want a coffee?" he asked. But he was out the door before Anyone could answer.

Phyllis shot me a quick "Hello" glare. I smiled.

"I told you she was strange," she said. And then she stared at me and I stared back, hard, attempting to bury the stare deep into her brain.

The Mother's face twisted behind her. She looked at me too, both of them looking, at the end of my bed. One mask angry, one mask sad.

"Mother, don't say that! Easter, it's not true. You're not strange."

And as she spoke that different person she'd become at the cabin began to disappear, melting off her frame and dripping to the ground, oozing along the maze of grout between the hospital-room tiles and out the door; her boob cup shirt looked silly and pathetic, her makeup clownish. She was the old Mother in the new Mother's uncomfortable costume, so she fidgeted as she spoke and shook her hair over her face.

"She *is* strange! I'm not saying I don't care for the girl, but she's strange, dear, and you know it as well as I. You remember what she did at my house."

"I didn't do that!" I yelped.

They both ignored me.

"She is not strange," The Mother said quietly.

"She is. Just like you were. Easter, you're going to go someplace to get the strange squeezed out of you, how would you like that?"

"She's not going anywhere unless she wants to, Mother!"

"Like hell. We're not making the same mistake twice, I'll tell you that much. I was too ashamed to send you somewhere and look how you turned out."

I sat there not saying anything. Get the strange squeezed out of me. Sounded easy enough. Suck Julia out. Suck what makes me special right out. And then I wished she wasn't already gone, because instead of her being dead forever I might have been able to just leave her there, at the place that sucks out strange, and still be able to see her whenever I wanted, at this place nearby enough but not home. A compromise.

"I would go to a place like that," I finally said.

It seemed to knock Phyllis back a bit; flakes of lacquer floated from her face to the floor like feathers. The Mother stood up.

"Really, Easter?" she said, dabbing her cry-blown cheeks with a wrinkled tissue. "Would you go someplace for a while? Do you think that would help? To be away?"
"I do."
"You're not strange, Easter."
"I know." I nodded. "Neither are you."

The Mother smiled. The tears had cooled her anger like summer rain long overdue.

Phyllis sat down, pulled a tube of lipstick from her purse, and applied it slowly, generously. I realized then that she'd be staying at The Lake House with The Mother and The Father that night, and I felt happy to be away from home already.

Mrs. Bellows' Apartment Building

And so, just as Julia predicted, I was sent to live somewhere else. A place for extraordinary girls on Princess Street, in a brick apartment building, blackened over the years by its proximity to the tire factory behind it. Princess Streets are everywhere, and this one wasn't unique for any reason. It was short and curved slightly to accommodate the used car dealership across the street. There was a convenience store on the corner run by three brothers who kept a pair of small, well-behaved dogs tied up out front. An oak tree lumbered in the front yard of the building and a broom leaning against a wicker chair collected dust on the small, square porch.

They sat me down in our most comfortable living room chair and told me all about the place. Phyllis had recommended it. The Mother spoke. She said things like "just for a little while" and "lovely facilities" and "a wonderful woman runs the place." She said things about Julia too, like "Julia makes you very sick, makes you do dangerous things, and we can't have her in our lives anymore."

I nodded and nodded and nodded. The Father stood behind The Mother, framed by the living room doorway, stirring a tall glass of chocolate milk with a straw. His eyes were across the street on a neighbor's house. He was convinced that there would be a party there tonight. Mayhem and loud music and underage drinking because the Fosters were up north for the weekend, leaving their pimpled son Barry to take care of the kitty litter and the ficus trees.

I looked up at him, focused on him as hard as he was focusing outside and all of a sudden, everything turned black around his shape and when I turned back to The Mother, everything was black around her shape too. She was still speaking, but her words sounded smothered and her mouth moved so slowly that it was hard to look at her. Her eyelids flapped lazy, like a drowsy baby's. In slow motion, every movement looks like such an effort.

A smile invaded her face and then slow motion dissolved as she noticed The Father peering even more intently through the glass, like a dog mesmerized by a squirrel. She squeezed her eyes shut, creases sprouting like I'd never seen before from the corners, so slowly slicing her skin. Then she pressed the knuckles of both hands into her eye sockets.

She'd been paying dearly for how she'd acted at The Lake

House. She was learning the consequences of treating The Father like that. Learning just how well he could ignore us. Her boob cup tops were hidden away in a closet somewhere, never to be seen again. I wondered what he'd said to her. How he'd corrected her. I wondered how horrible she felt.

The blackness around them was so dense, I felt as though I could scoop out a shelf and rest The Father's chocolate milk on it. Cut out a tiny hole and shove The Mother inside.

But I kept nodding and nodding. I looked up, past The Mother, beyond The Father's leering profile, through the door-frame, and saw Julia for a split second listening at the top of the stairs, crouching behind the spindles, her long arms hanging over the banister. But then she disappeared. Just a ghost. The look on her face made me shiver.

And without warning, color was restored to The House, regular speeds resumed, and The Mother was still speaking:

"We love you very much, Easter. Very, very much. We'll be here for you."

The apartment building on Princess St. was a special place for sick girls. But girls who were just barely sick, or not even really sick at all, just sad and lonely and strange. Not quite crazy enough to be drooling and comatose in a loony bin. But close. Teetering on the brink of happiness and wanting badly to stay for good. That was one of the stipulations of living at Mrs. Bellows' Apartment Building. You had to want to stay for good. Stay happy, that is. And normal. And I didn't know how I could be normal with Julia around.

The Parents dropped me off on a Sunday afternoon. The Mother was feeling all out of whack, squirrely, because she was supposed to have been soaking still in the tub for hours already. When I stepped out of the car, she stepped out too and stood looking at me, her face twisting up slowly, out of her control, and she leapt forward and hugged me tight. The Father'd squeezed my shoulder before I got out of the car and sat, engine running, in Mrs. Bellow's driveway. The Mother whispered things in my ear.

"I love you, Easter, so, so much. I love you. I'll see you as often as I can, okay?"

Her voice shook. In a series of enormous kisses she transferred all the wetness on her face along my neck and up to my cheek.

I could tell she was scared. Scared to be all alone in The House. And I realized for the first time that she didn't have a friend in the world. That with me gone, she'd have no one to talk to at all. So I hugged her back. As tight as I could.

"Don't worry, Mom," I whispered into her ear.

I was her Julia, her only friend and Tooth House companion; the only other person in the world who knew all the same secret things that she did.

Somehow my body found the give for her momentarily

tighter squeeze just before she let go and held me an arm's length away by the shoulders.

"You're not strange," she said again.

And then they were gone.

There were many rules in place at Mrs. Bellows' Apartment Building, general rules as well as rules that were particular to each season-themed room. I lived in the June Room, decorated in the yellow and green colors of early summer. A rule particular to this room was that you weren't allowed to pick at the chipping paint on the walls and if you couldn't help it, then Mrs. Bellows would be forced to duct-tape oven mitts over your hands, an empty threat that she thought was a funny thing to say to the girls who moved into this room. I could tell she'd used the line a million times before.

There was also a December Room, which was white and gray. One had to be particularly clean to live in the December Room, on account of how stainable it was. The August Room was blue and contained a radiator that required special attention. The October Room was orange and red and one had to be sure to keep the curtains open at all times on sunny winter days because it was from the large windows in the October room that Mrs. Bellows liked to bring extra heat to that part of the building.

Mrs. Bellows kept an immaculate record of the comings and goings at her place. Visitors had to be on a special list kept behind the reception desk and outings had to be detailed to Mrs. Bellows and approved. She had a cabinet full of medicine behind the front desk too, separated into four compartments for each of the girls who lived there. Each compartment was characterized by a unique skyline of pills and syringes required to keep each of the girls on their own separate roads to recovery.

Three times a day, at exactly twelve o'clock, three o'clock, and six o'clock, Mrs. Bellows would make her rounds, administering the correct medications to the correct girls. Mostly sedatives and vitamins.

The sedatives made me feel like I was floating: lying on my back, unable to move, sliced vertically, half of my body submerged in black water that filled my ears with loud nothing. The liquid slithered calmly most of the time, the sort of warm, tepid environment that scuttling, soft-bellied creatures thrive and multiply in. Sometimes the residual ripples of a big wave somewhere in the distance would cause the water to seep into my mouth from the sides, and the weight of it would make me sink, my nostrils and eye sockets spilled into with thick black. My head the first to go under, followed by my neck and chest. The water rubbed me always. Mrs. Bellows usually arrived in time to pull me up by the elbow. I wanted her to let me keep sinking, wave goodbye to my pale, wide-eyed face obscured by the ripples in the water.

Mrs. Bellows was very, very old, with short, stubby limbs and a curved back. The best description I could possibly offer is this: she looked like a tortoise with a gray wig on its head. And bright pink lipstick that trickled along the wrinkles from her lips like little rivers. Frankly, I found her sort of terrifying to look at. Every time our eyes stuck together, I moved mine away very quickly. I looked at the chipped paint on the ceiling or the cracked tiles on the floor, or the dickhead cat or the Victorian drapes, or whatever. When we first met she'd been working on a cross-stitch poem, only one line visible: "These busy insects are eating away."

I furrowed my brow at it and she noticed and told me it was written by her favorite poet, and that it was hard to find the right color green because so many of them look like puke and not springtime, and about how she wanted to put it on a pillow, but would likely frame it instead because it's more sanitary than a fancy pillow you can never properly wash.

The other girls called her "the Gatekeeper."

The Parents visited whenever they were allowed to: The Mother, driving over and assembling big dinners in the crockpot early in the morning before either of us was awake. Folding our laundry and putting little braids in our hair while we slept so that when we woke up and took them out we'd look like long-disregarded Barbie dolls. The Father evidenced his visits with piles of change and receipts left on the coffee table and streaks in the carpet next to the bed where he'd rubbed his feet. I don't remember it well but I know The Father came once alone. I read it in the visitor's book.

Mrs. Bellows had decorated each of the rooms herself. Hand-me-downs or garage sale treasures with long, boring stories attached. Us girls were allowed to bring our own duvets and mine was brand new, top of the line, filled with something even more soft and squishy than baby feet.

I usually sat on the couch in my room, limbs sprawled out strategically as pipes to maximize comfort. I'd watch TV for hours and hours and hours and hours, rolling toward a bowl of chips for another handful or into the bathroom for a quick pee during commercial breaks. Sitting, sitting, sitting, glorious sitting. The feeling of loose legs, tingling, hanging over the arm of a chair, or feet elevated by pillows, whole body as still as sleep but the brain still focused, eyes still open. I love television. I'm so glad that I wasn't born two hundred years ago when there were outhouses and no television and everything was an enormous inconvenience.

I watched a channel that played sitcoms all day long and I'd yet to see a repeat. My brain had started to introduce canned laughter into my day-to-day activities. If I gagged myself while brushing my tongue in the morning, a dry retch moving through me like lightning, the roar of a cackling audience trapped in a tin drum filled my ears.

In sitcoms, every house looks the way that houses are supposed to: open and comfortable with no secrets or shadows or shameful bits, no closed rooms or dark corners that company can't be allowed near. The upstairs is the same as the main floor, which is the same as the basement, all accessible and clean and open for viewing. And every room is neatly cluttered, perfectly representing the acceptably offbeat family that lives there.

It seemed odd to me that they never showed the television in sitcoms. Televisions were always in front of the garish sitcom couch that faced out toward us. Tucked neatly into the only spot in the house not viewable. But the characters would sit and stare at it from time to time; in effect, stare at me. It was as if watching the television, viewing these acceptably offbeat families with their wide-open houses and secret-less existences, taking them in as a possibility of how people live, was the same as being watched ourselves somehow. And it felt that way. A two-way street. I guess it's too much to ask that watching be one-sided. That's not really fair. The more you watch, the more you're watched, and that's the way that it should be, I guess. But I still couldn't quite figure out who it was watching me.

Another Squirrel

When the first coil of cigarette smoke ensnared my nose, I imagined it had a life of its own. Like magic from a wand. The sun had made its way behind me, finally, so the front of the rock was brightly lit and as bare as a canvas, the smoke casting a willowy shadow across it, replenished a few times over with fresh lungfuls. I looked up and my eyes followed the smoke deeper into The Woods, where it had rambled around the thick arms of trees and hopped from leaf to leaf and bud to bud, which were as round and pink as gumballs and blurred the jutting lines of the branches. It came to a concentrated point at the end of a long white cigarette in the claws of a little squirrel. The same little squirrel I'd seen eating the hamburger a few minutes or hours ago. Gray. A fluctuation of black and white like a snowy television set.

It was sitting up straight in the skirt of collected skin over its feet, looking at me. It then set its sights on the scroll of smoke that had made its way to my nose and with a hop began to follow it. Around branches, over leaves, under buds, skewering the smoke through the center with its wet nose until he was right up against my nose.

He tossed the cigarette in the pool of blood that had collected next to my hip and then stuck his little hands out, rolled up the skin on his arms, and dipped them into it. When he pulled them out they were drenched with red. He did the same to his feet. Then, without warning, he scurried up the rock, leaving a trail of little prints all around it. Returned to the inkwell, re-soaked his quills, and began the process again. He did this four more times and finally, the last time, he didn't return from the dark side of the rock. I stared at the little red prints, stared and stared and stared until they became a picture. A picture of The Terrible Thing, right there in front of me. I squeezed my eyes shut, hoping to lose the picture the way that images in clouds can be lost if you close your eyes and think of something else.

And I suddenly wished that I could have been born as ink on paper. Printed. Because then I would know that I was really here. Because there I was. A hieroglyph in a cave, chiseled with iron or fingered in blood, etched into stone or scratched into a tree. I wanted to be a print on the rock.

To be a print on the rock. A print on the rock. Five little squirrel fingers and toes, red rippling bumps, red footprints all over, two hundred, two hundred, two hundred, counted three times: two hundred, and all exactly the same. Two hundred prints on the rock. Things that could be counted were very special to me now. I'd counted leaves and twigs and birds today, understanding The Woods by its numbers.

Counting the seconds before the sun was almost all the way down. And The Woods took on the cold, metallic quality of dusk. It must be getting close to six o'clock. The Mother would have wondered where I went by now.

And I wouldn't mind being found, either. It was getting dark and cold and I didn't want to be out here after the sun went down and the nighttime critters that feast on bleeding things came out. I thought I saw a pair of eyes between two slim trees.

"Hello?" I croaked.

A few seconds passed.

"Hello? Is someone out there?"

I hate the fuzz that grows over everything at dusk, that frosty gray blurriness that makes you feel like you've got to get your eyes checked or that everything has suddenly started to foam.

"Please, if someone's out there, could you step out? I'd like to go home now."

No one emerged. Maybe next time I saw the squirrel I'd ask it to go get help. But I wasn't expecting to see another one. Fuzzy things tend to clear out when it gets dark.

I looked down at the blackness spread all the way up my

shorts. I could feel the stiffness at my waist. I would soon be a tiny figurine, like one of Mr. Ungula's, and he could stick me wherever he wanted. Forever. Looking in the same direction, at the same collection of crotchety trees, decorated with old sneakers and rags and foils and wrappers and cups thrown from cars zipping along the highway. I hated the way they seemed to lean on each other like a battalion of elderly war heroes, demonstrating camaraderie for a photo. And they were in on it, too; they could have entertained me if they'd wanted to, but they didn't. They were just standing around being boring. So I hated them.

Even though it felt like hours, it's possible that I'd only been here for twenty or thirty minutes, minutes becoming little lifetimes. But I had to have been lying here for longer than just half an hour because I just had to have been. The thought of not knowing, the *possibility* that I might have only been lying here for a few minutes, snatched the breath from my throat. My lungs felt like they were being squeezed shut, pulled closed as though by strings on a hood, tighter, smaller, harder to breathe. I couldn't be stuck like this anymore. I couldn't be trapped. My breath kept getting caught up in my throat, sticky, swollen, barely getting through without a loud wheeze. I could feel something horrific bubbling, some reaction worse than crying or screaming, even worse than vomiting.

Furry creatures with flat fingernails and feisty little teeth gnawing on the cords that connected my eyes to my brain.

Short circuits running through my body, sirens going off

everywhere, even in dark corners behind slacker organs that never see any real action, like the spleen, who was able to rub the sleep from his eyes just in time to look busy and see all the other organs in a veritable tizzy. The hardworking organs freaking out. Father organs kissing their families goodbye, leaving gooey, crying children behind, then sliding down my bones like fireman's poles, off to work to figure out where the problem was coming from. None of them would ever suspect the snappy, nervous, belligerent little critters making mince of my eye wiring, disconnecting them from the world but not blinding me.

What happens when eyes still work, operate just fine, but are no longer connected to the brain? Something worse than vomit is what happens.

And for my poor innards, having no idea what was going on behind my eyes, no knowledge of the furry, flat-nailed creatures and their feisty teeth, there had to be some other reason. The worker bits in the vomit room were sweating buckets. They'd pressed the vomit button fifteen minutes ago; something should be gurgling by now, WHY WASN'T ANYTHING GURGLING?? Quick, get Walter on the phone in Guts. I can't get him, sir! Well, keep trying! My cells were praying, gathering up close together, waiting for the new, worse-than-vomit thing to happen.

Another minute passed, another island of consciousness traversed or maybe two islands or three or forty-five. I was making sounds. I'm not sure for how long. I had a big breath in my lungs and was releasing tiny, croaking spurts of it through the very back of my throat, like hostages.

Controlling this voice that was so different from my own.

These spurts started to sound like a word, a name that I'd been thinking of all day:

> "Lev, Lev, Lev, Lev, Lev, Lev, Lev, Lev, Lev, Lev, Lev, Lev, Lev, Lev."

But I was sure he couldn't hear me, sure he was somewhere on Princess street, in bed, in his bug-filled basement room that smelled of cold and hair, or at his parents' dinner table slurping up subterranean humanoid mush, or even walking to the Miniature Wonderland to see me. He couldn't be The Something Coming, here to push the rock and hoist me up and save me from The Terrible Thing. No one was coming. I'd be all alone forever.

I decided that I should become evil then. Wait for someone else to come traipsing along the path, lure them close, then catch them and hold them so they'd have to keep me company forever. I'm the bad guy. The undead. The demon. The evil thing lurking in The Woods, making it unsafe for young girls to wander. And actually it was better this way because now I never had to worry about bad guys ever again. I'm the bad guy. And the odds of there being two bad guys in The Woods at one time were pretty slim, I think.

Easter Story

The Mother always said that without powder, she was nothing but a hunk of meat. A steak flayed from a carcass, and once flayed, entitled to its own anatomy. As a steak she had an identifiable T-bone and a relative weight and a particular marbling pattern. Easter liked the idea of a part being cut from the whole and turning into something else all together. A callous sliced from the soft tissue of a mollusk becomes a pearl. A parasite cut out of a woman becomes a person.

But everyone is just flesh, warmed by a heart pumping blood through organized veins and into and out of internal organs. To The Mother, this wasn't an existence at all. A hunk of meat isn't alive unless it's understood differently, as something separate from the flesh it was cut from. Understood in the way that it's supposed to be understood. As a rib eye or a porterhouse or filet mignon. So The Mother wore her powder and existed in the world as a Beautiful Woman with a little lucky dice nose.

She was fanatical about it. Compulsive. Blossoms of blush brushes lay aside dishes of bone-colored powder on just about every flat surface in The House. On the tops of bookshelves, windowsills, and end tables, brushes relaxed, idle, waited to be plucked by The Mother for a quick swipe or circle or smush. The areas surrounding the powder dishes were always covered in a film of barely there dust, perfect to drag a finger along or flatten a hand into or leave messages like the ever popular "wash me." Before she left The House, she had to be sure that she'd dusted herself over with powder, allowed it to settle on her shape and indicate her perimeters. A little lipstick as well. Always a little lipstick. She wouldn't want to go out with an invisible mouth.

Clouds of unpredictable particles, invisible in the air but visible on clothes and in hair, billowed around The Mother all the time and Easter was terrified of any landing on her. It was too soft, too absent. Between her fingers it felt like nothing. But it was definitely something. Easter wondered how old The Mother had been when she'd first put on the powder, first realized that she was a shade without it. First understood that she needed it to exist in the world in the same way that she needed just enough food and water and a warm bed to sleep in. Maybe she left The House one day and no one noticed her and she thought for a moment that she might have died in her sleep that night. That is, until she smashed a jar of spaghetti sauce in the international foods section at the grocery store or bumped into a surly old man on the bus, and then people noticed her. But not in a good way. She wanted to be noticed in a good way.

So she bought a tablet of packed tight, bone-colored powder and brushed herself all over so you could see her perfectly well, or at least a shell of powder perfectly well. And a pair of lips. And the more she wore this mask of talc and ground fish scales, the more invisible she became underneath. Every night when she wiped it all off, the face that stared back was more and more nothing.

Would Easter reach an age when she didn't hate the powder? An age when it stopped making her feel chilly all down her spine? Or would she simply start disappearing? Wake up one day and wonder if she'd died because no one noticed her. Not that it sounded bad. Not to be noticed. It would be nice not to be noticed, the way that people didn't notice Julia. But she didn't want to start something like that, applying the powder, without being sure. Because she still wasn't totally clear on what came first: the absence, or the powder.

The June Room

She couldn't sleep and the other girls probably couldn't either. The thought of all of those people not sleeping, just lying frustrated in their beds: breathing heavily, perfectly tucked in, arms over blankets outlining their bodies; impressions of four torsos in four separate rooms through four floral bedspreads. Holes bored into ceilings from the glare of eight still eyes. They were all awake but not moving, reaching desperately for sleep as it drifted further away. The harder she stared, the more her walls began to look like they were covered in bugs, alive with bugs, throbbing with scuttling, slimy bugs. The same bugs she'd flicked off Lev, the same bugs that invaded his underground lair. Every one of them sucking the life from her daffodil paint. She was stiff as a statue, eyes round and wide and vulnerable, cracked bowls brimming with fear. Her palms splayed out on the comforter beside her concrete body, warming it with worry and dampening it with sweat.

What were the rules here?
Could they leave the walls?

Would they touch her?

No, they couldn't leave the walls unless she looked at them. When she looked at them they could come closer. So all she had to do was not look at them. That should be easy enough. When her eyes closed, something began to happen. A sound from the deep dark of her head. A single bell. Small and held between two thick fingers, their nails as big as coins. The bell's shapely body, limp-looking and exhausted as a plucked flower; the clapper gliding against the petals and sending a shudder rather than a shock through the round silvery lip.

Just barely singing but growing louder, slowly moving over the ripples of her brain like warm water, starting to move faster and faster until it kept perfect time with the bugs' pattering little feet. They almost fed off of each other, faster and faster and faster, agitated and extending their perimeters, moving closer to the bed.

The bell was calling them. The bell from The Tooth House doors, the bell she heard when Lev was near, made these bugs writhe nearer.

So she had to stop. Stop thinking of the bell. Just go to sleep, kill the bell. But the bell was persistent. And it liked the shapes the bugs put themselves in, the order they brought to their frenzied crawling. She looked out the window and calmed herself down by finding shapes in the stars. The sky hadn't changed the whole time she'd been in the apartment building, so the stars were a scene she knew inside and out, a scene upon which any number of stories could be played comfortably. Familiar faces and objects, the same you'd find in patterned wallpaper or hardwood panelling after the lights are off.

But she could still hear them, scuttling feet along her springtime paint, like tiny pebbles falling into a tin can from the puckered circle of a slowly opening hand.

Segments ribbing against segments; the crackle of an old record; a bustling street; the lub-dub of a ceiling fan; a consistent complement upon which other sounds may fall nicely.

Flecks of dried bug skin probably hemmed the room, falling to the floor in a graceful zigzag like snowflakes. She could smell them, too: the brisk, sour smell of cold blood. Wall-to-wall-to-wall-to-wall bugs. The thought of their feet on her skin wrung her with anxious nausea.

Quivering eyelids closed over wild eyeballs. Paddleball heartbeat, awake beneath the costume of sleep.

Sorry

The front porch at Mrs. Bellows' Apartment Building had a wicker rocking chair that caught the breeze easily, like a kind of squeaking wind chime. I'd already squeaked away a million seconds that day when Lev walked right into my line of sight and stopped in the dead center of it. Lev, who'd told me long ago that he lived somewhere along Princess Street. Lev, who I'd said I didn't like anymore.

I squeak squeak squeaked without saying hello.
He broke the silence.

"Hi," he said.
"Did you follow me?" I asked.
"You really hurt my feelings."
"I'm sorry."
"At first I really wanted to hurt your feelings back," he said. "Then I saw that you'd moved in here, and I thought maybe you didn't mean to hurt my feelings."

"No, maybe I didn't really want to."

"Why'd you do it?"

"I don't want to talk about it." And I turned my head and continued squeaking.

"What are you doing in here?"

"That's a very personal question, you know."

And when he looked down at his peeking feet I saw a little bug scuttle across his head and slip into the collar of his shirt. The same little bug that made the walls of the June Room froth. And then I heard the bell again; it rang lightly, thrummed along the lip instead of banged.

"I'm really am sorry," I said.

And he lifted his head and two more little bugs that had been hiding beneath the epaulets of his jacket lifted their antennaed heads with him. I noticed that they moved in the pockets of his jacket, too; I could trace their outlines moving over each other excitedly. The bell got louder.

"It's okay. You're not working anymore, I hear."

"Who'd you hear that from?"

"I went looking for you at the Wonderland. Mr. Ungula chased me away with a broom. He said you had enough problems without me sniffing after you."

I laughed and the bell got louder still, making it hard to see for a minute, everything all blurry. Then Lev, still smiling, took a step back. He disappeared from his clothes, which kept his shape for a split second and then crumpled to the ground in a whoosh. Solid cylinders of writhing bugs scurried from the arms and legs of his clothes like water from hoses. I closed my eyes tight and opened them again and there he was. Lev. Standing like normal, not transformed into a thousand bugs at all.

"There's not a lot that would stop me following you around, Easter," he said quietly.
"What do you mean?"
"I mean, you can tell me why you're here if you want. It won't change my wanting to follow you."

I smiled and stood up and moved to the middle porch step. He moved to the middle porch step too. The road-map veins under his translucent skin turned my stomach a bit. He held his hand out for me to put mine in, knuckles down so I could see his toad-belly palms. And they felt as cold as toad bellies, too. But maybe it was nice. Because toad bellies are better than nothing.

The June Room

She remembered now what happened. What happened was that Seisyll came knocking on The Parents' door with a plastic bag of dead cat in one hand and a familiar red ribbon in the other. She hid in the living room, under a woolly gray blanket that rarely moved from its casually tossed perch on the arm of the chair, but really, there was nothing casual about it. Its function was to hide a large, unfixable gash in the upholstery, and more importantly, to keep her and her sister from picking at the irresistibly fluffy guts spilling out, which they both had a tendency to do. The same went for rips in the wallpaper or snags in the carpet. The back of the couch was pushed against a wall of tall windows and if she lifted her head just a bit she could get a good peek at the front lawn.

The night was a picture, smoothed tightly over stiff matting and framed by the cream-colored molding that accented their living room windows back then. A pattern of whining cats occupied the image; they decorated the grass and kneaded the oak tree and, like little bread crumbs, a trail of them led up the porch and stopped behind Seisyll's crispy, exposed heels. Of course, she couldn't see the heels, but she knew what they looked like. She knew what he was wearing without having to see him. She knew how his snarling face moved as he barked at The Mother, who had opened the door only as much as she had to; enough to hear him and let him see her face, but not enough to let his steam billow in and curl the wallpaper. Which she and her sister would only make worse with their incessant picking.

After a few minutes The Mother closed the door and walked into the dark living room. She said, "Easter, honey, did you hear what Seis said?" And Easter nodded. And she nodded and she nodded and she nodded until she was sobbing and she wasn't sure when the nodding turned into sobbing but it had and she'd buried her face into The Mother's neck and The Mother rubbed her back, her palm up and down and up and down, moving Easter's shirt around, squeezing her tight, and for some reason Easter opened her mouth and bit The Mother's throat hard; a tendon slipped between her smooth teeth. The Mother screamed and pushed her away and grabbed her neck and shrieked, "Why on earth would you do that?" and Easter ran up the stairs and thought to herself "Because I'm evil, that's why. I'm an evil monster, two at once all the time and both evil. That's why."

And the betrayed faces of the little cats scrolled along the back of her closed eyelids this evening as she lay quietly in the June Room in Mrs. Bellows' Apartment Building. The bugs hadn't made it off the walls yet, but they were close. She had grown lazy, or curious *maybe. What would happen if she let them touch her? Sometimes she let herself indulge in the craving for a long antennae flicking at her toes, which were as red as cranberries all winter. Maybe she craved the feeling of cold, dead heaviness writhing over her cemented thighs; her whole body benumbed with a fear, not of their presence, but that her movement might frighten them away.*

She opened her eyes and saw something in her window: cats, a shade left behind, printed momentarily onto the real world from the picture etched onto the backs of her eyelids.

But as her vision adjusted, she realized her error. Those weren't cats out the window, complementing her stars. They were bugs, crawling all over the sky as though it were made of nylon, filling up the window, invading her eyes. And once they were in there, she couldn't close her eyes without seeing the bugs, so she was always watching and they would always be moving closer. And from her eyes, they began to invade other spots, too, empty spaces where memories had been, or should have been. Spots where Julia usually was. Where she'd wrenched things out and filled them up with her stories. Where she'd tinkered and adjusted and made things right. Where The Father might have been if he weren't a black hole. The bugs, implants but not. Smoothing things over, rubbing them down. Brain etched into. Worn by scribbling feet. So that every implant went as unnoticed as a bone in the body.

The June Room

One evening, Mrs. Bellows knocked on her door. It was time to go to the Craft Room where three other girls would be, ready to stitch things and paint things and watch things dry. They sat in the same spots each time, a pair on either side of a long wooden table, each perched on a spinning stool that seemed to sprout from the ground like a toadstool. Easter didn't want to go. She'd spent the whole morning trying to come up with excuses, but Mrs. Bellows knew everything she did, knew that she'd be lying. There was no getting out of it. Mrs. Bellows seemed to detect the anxiety creeping from Easter like an odor.

She said, "You can be the scissor boss, Easter."

As though that would make her feel better.

When she walked in, they all looked up at her. Three other girls, pale skin, long hair, eyes wide. They each spun slightly on their stools, left and right and left and right and left and right, and wadded thread into heaped nests in front of them; the spools *rattled, loud as door stoppers. Impaled and spinning on well-placed nails, as deeply rooted as totem poles into the pocked crafts table.*

The spools generated an endless hum, a mindless buzz to smother the quiet. Fingers worked quickly at bits of quilt, moving against each other like puppies after a teat: untangling, pulling, threading, nourishing themselves with busy purpose, organizing the thread into things identifiable. Things with names: ducks, roses, cherries, leaves, sailboats, a small hive of buzzing worker bees; producing new things for the world from a set of widely distributed instructions. They pierced and picked and dug and tightened and stitched their new things to life.

The Craft Room walls were covered in old quilts made by far-away, presumably cured, ex-tenants. Images of health: a Thanksgiving-themed quilt hung heavy on the north wall: families at a table, the backs of their heads a furious, concentrated zigzag of brown and yellow thread; a steaming turkey excreting stuffing from its crisp rectum; a bowl of mashed potatoes as blindingly white as a diaper. On the south wall hung an army of coarse, felted faces, patrolling the room, peeking over shoulders, alerting Mrs. Bellows when the girls were acting up. Each face looked like a character from "Guess Who?" A fat, yellow-haired policeman, face dimpled and boyish; a red-headed lady with big blue glasses and a straw hat with a cornucopia spilling out on top of it.

These displayed creations were supposed to be inspiration for the girls: become healthy, want it, produce, produce, produce! The ability and desire to produce copies, to reproduce, makes you a healthy young thing. And they all wanted to be healthy young things. Otherwise they wouldn't be there.

Easter sat down. Mrs. Bellows handed her the scissors carefully and she held them tight in her hands, clasping their jaws shut. Apparently it was a great honor to be trusted with such a dangerous instrument, trusted to do all of the snipping for the entire day. And it was an honor, too, for the scissors, as they were pretty sure that no other pair of scissors in the world were as highly coveted as they were, represented such an enormous responsibility. How many other pairs of scissors could claim to be a tool toward recovery? Well, maybe lots, but none that these scissors knew.

"Could you cut this thread for me?" one girl asked.

She had a small gummy smile and red cheeks. Another girl walked up and held a string to be severed in front of her face, too jealous to formulate a polite request. Easter preferred this. The thought of people being so jealous of her made her guts tickle. She would stick her fingers slowly through the scissor's holes and spread them wide open, proud like a peacock tail. Then with a rehearsed casualness, she would snip the thread or the yarn or the fabric that had been held before her. It was fun to be the scissor boss.

She looked at each of the girls. Hunched over, their thin, restless fingers became as long and sharp as needles, probing and diving over and under the vast stretches of cream-colored fabric. When did it happen that their fingers became needles? Needles of bone. She'd heard that somewhere before. Read it in a book that made her cry. Long, sharp, white, tapered needles. Filled with marrow, or tooth pulp.

Had her fingers become needles as well? She looked at her own dry-knuckled hand, splayed out and flattened on the table. Just a hand, with regular, pliable fingers. But theirs weren't. And now their eyes looked like buttons, smooth and blank behind hair that hung in front of their poreless plastic faces like yarn from their soft skulls, pooling on the table in swirls like sleeping snakes. This must be what the world looked like with no Julia. This must be normal.

She leaned over and stole a snip of yarn from one of the girl's heads. The girl shrieked, her mouth a flat, oblong section of black velvet. She pointed a needled finger at Easter and began manipulating her black velvet mouth, screaming something about the culprit being dangerous. Easter tried to understand, but she couldn't hear the voice all smothered in black velvet.

But that girl's finger, pointing. How nice it would be to have that finger, that needle finger, sneak it back to her room to keep, to cross-stitch a little picture of a bug into her own skin. Easter leapt up onto the table and grabbed the girl's arm, pinning her hand down beneath her knee while the girl screamed louder and flailed about with the rest of her body. Easter drove her knee harder into the girl's palm, said "SHUT UP!" and tried to position the scissors to cut the needle finger right off. She was suddenly grabbed by the wrist and pulled to the ground and made to eat sleeping pills and lie in bed.

But even with the sleeping pills she couldn't sleep. Not with all these bugs around. She'd been staring at them since they'd forced their way onto her sky. Eyes closed crawling bugs, eyes open crawling bugs. She would let her eyes bury themselves, become wedged between their muscular bodies, roll around like marbles as the bugs grazed against one another. She stared until they didn't even look like bugs anymore, they became the shapes of anything she wanted, like mashed potato clouds emblazoned by sunny days.

The bell, louder than it had ever been before, appeared in her mind. Her face reflected on the smooth, silver bell. The reflection small, contained, not at all like on the back of a spoon, over which it spread like a creamy infection.

On the bell, her face was a freckle, a tiny spot, a blister on a bud, a throbbing sac of larvae that ached to burst.

She stuck out her pink tongue and the little imperfection mimicked. It was just like her but smaller, rounder; the world on the bell is a world without corners. Her lips spread apart, an opening the size of a pencil eraser.

She breathed a cloud of hot breath onto the bell; bleach, powder, paint; a fog to hide her imperfection reflection. It tingled barely, a wind chime just gripped still by the thick of summer.

And she was gone, hidden behind a picture of her breath. With her smallest finger she pressed a circle into the fog, a clear moment for her tiny face. The imperfection. A boil, a pimple, something to be treated, dried up, picked off, burned and buffed out. A smooth, pure bud. Once again, she slowly coated the bell in breath and rubbed and rubbed and rubbed. But she couldn't seem to get to her face again. She wished she'd said good-bye.

It rang so clear, so loud, unceasing. Once an implant, a foreign object, placed there in her brain and over the doors by The Mother, but now as organic as the bugs had become.

Two warm tears squeezed out of the corners of her tightly compressed eyelids, riding along a particularly prominent crease in the pillowcase. A warm, wet patch of white fabric. She squeezed her eyes even tighter, as tight as they could be, and rolled her cheek into the wetness, the sound of the ocean in a seashell crashing against her ear drums. This was stupid. She couldn't bear this all night. She let her left eye crack open just a bit and she looked out the window. A clear night. The stars looked like a thousand pinpricks in a stretch of black fabric, snags in a pair of hearty tights. She remembered borrowing her mother's too-long nylons: they hung over her toes like elf shoes, got caught on nails in the hardwood floor at the party. They were garbage after that. The Father pulled them off, rolled them up, and threw them in the trash. She wanted to find a loose thread in the twilight. Pull it. See what shined so brightly behind it, through the snags. She shut her eyes tight again and a word drifted onto the backs of her eyelids:
Lonely.
The bugs ebbed around her bed, creaming against the skirt.
Lonely.
She felt weight tugging down at the edges of her sheets, pulling down tight over her body.
The waves churned in her ears.

The loneliest girl.

Heaviness on top of her, the gentle thud of fingers keeping time on a blanket.

But you don't have to be lonely.

A million tiny feet tapping, little bodies scraping against her crisp sheets.

You've got a million friends.

She opened her eyes and crawling over the corners of her bed were thousands and thousands of bugs. And the bell rang so loud, so constant that it became like traffic in a city, like the crackle of a record, a ceiling fan lub-dubbing; there and meant to be there and even strange without it.

They can live inside you and make you not alone.

They crawled over each other, under each other, moved together like thick, black oil, about to envelop her.

Should let them stay.

They were all over her, covered her like a quilt. She tried to scream but as soon as she opened her mouth, they moved together like liquid and filled it up, scurried down her throat, tickling her from the inside out, touching her all over. She could barely breathe. All over her face the cold ripple of their segmented bodies moved up and down. They rubbed at her as though she were a piece of beach glass, made opaque, smooth, numb, wearing away all of her edges. In the bell, a world without corners.

Time to Leave The Woods

It was 7:30. The Mother would have been doing the thing that worried mothers do on TV—sitting at the table with her hands wrapped around a mug. She'd have poured herself a cup of warm something, groping at it without drinking, wearing something loose, seemingly thrown on in a fit of terror but still flattering. She would wonder if I'd told her about a place I'd go on a warm June night. Wonder and wonder and then feel guilty that she couldn't remember.

I was ready for someone to come and find me. Quite ready in fact. Gray dusk was fast becoming black night. Half of the planet behind a closed eyelid. I couldn't escape the things coming for me. Creatures crawling out of real, woodsy dark to feast on the dead; or in my case, what they wrongfully believed to be dead.

I am dead. I died a few hours ago, my body as still as any other corpse, but I just didn't realize it. That's why it's been so hard for me to look around. My whole body held still by a big, cold hand closed tight around me, white and smooth, skin hanging over tendons like a wet towel over a rack, nails long and crisp as corn flakes. This hand held me still and quiet and I couldn't fight it. *I* am a figurine and *I* am trapped inside. Finally, after all of these hours, I'm completely made of wood.

While all around me the dark world had devoured everything. Finished off The Woods as I knew them, about to enter my whole body the way that it enters a sleeping hand. Filling me up with stillness. The trees around me began to quiver, losing their drive to remain inanimate. The darkness licked its lips, tasting up the forest floor, drinking from my pool of blood. Shadows growing, spreading like a disease, and the things that had been restricted by their borders would be able to move freely.

The occasional headlight brought a distorted wave of illumination into my world. It was different out there. Things would know that I was dead. New sounds bounced off the trees; owls, heavy winds forcing their way loudly between branches, increasingly aggressive bugs burrowing their way toward me, picking at me too eagerly, a squabbling sound below. I hope I'm still alive. I hope I haven't been feasted on yet. Footsteps crunched somewhere near. The Something Coming.

A car went by, momentarily illuminating everything. I thought I saw them grab Something with their light. Those eyes again, peeking from between trees. Closer this time. Then complete darkness.

"Hello? Hello? If someone is out there, please help me, my legs are stuck under this rock. I've been bleeding for hours and hours, please. I don't want to be here anymore!"

It was The Something Coming. It was finally here. Now that the dark world had enveloped me entirely, The Something Coming felt safe enough to show itself. I don't care what it is. I don't care. Be whatever you want, Something Coming, I need a change anyway.

Another car went by and I screamed at the top of my lungs, thinking that someone inside might hear me. They must not have. Because they didn't stop. Maybe I really was already dead. Maybe I wasn't making a sound at all. Were my lips moving? Were they? I moved them around, stuck my tongue out, made loud, bizarre squeaks, growled. Was I making a sound? I couldn't tell anymore. Then everything seemed to go silent. Nothing rustled or chirped. I became deaf, blind, trapped in the smooth white hand that had become like a box, the exact size and shape of my body. I pounded and squirmed and clawed at the box. Scratched and tore until I'd left my fingernails somewhere along the gouges. The silence was decimating me.

But then I wasn't blind. And I wasn't in any box either. My fingernails were still intact. Another pair of headlights definitely illuminated a flash of red in the trees. Hair, perhaps? A bright, unnatural red. Someone was out there.

"Hello, hello, HELLO! I know you're there. I know you're there, I saw you! Now help me with this stupid rock or there'll be trouble. I'll tell everyone that I was dying under a rock and you didn't help me."

Another car went by and the eyes emerged from behind the tree. A whole body topped with red hair made its way out of the shadows toward me. It was Julia. I guess she'd decided to come back for me after all.

"Hi Easter," she said, as she walked slowly toward me.

The look on her face had The Terrible Thing written all over it.

"So you found it."
"Yeah. I found it."
"What are we gonna do?" I asked.

It's the thing I'd wanted to ask her all along. The thing that she would have eventually pried out of me had she not crushed me with a rock instead and took off for The House.

She shrugged. I closed my eyes and saw The Terrible Thing:

Easter was able to sneak out pretty easily this morning. She knew that if she wasn't gone when Mrs. Bellows woke up she'd have to answer for whatever came over her in the Craft Room last night. The bad thing she'd been about to do all on her own, without Julia to blame.

She changed into warmer clothes, stepped slowly out of the room (careful to avoid the creaks she knew so well), grabbed the bike from the side of the building, and rode it all the way home. Wind whipping her gripped white knuckles, so tight on the handlebars that they began to ache before she reached The Tooth House. Her key fit in the lock. There was no reason it shouldn't, but she wasn't sure. Mrs. Bellows had said that they should have controlled contact with one another, scheduled visits only. That The Parents needed to solve their own problems before Easter came back. She said, "You should really find one another again." And for some reason that had caused Easter to burst out laughing and The Mother cried and The Father barely moved, like callouses formed into the couch.

The Parents would still be sleeping, for at least a while. Easter crept up the stairs and straight into the bathroom, aching to stare at herself in a way that she couldn't in the shared bathrooms at Mrs. Bellows' Apartment Building.

But The Tooth House Bathroom was cold, unlike it had ever been before. Cold and still and simultaneously empty and full like the air before first lightning cracks. The shower curtain was pulled shut, so she opened it.

The Mother lay still as a reptile in the tub. The red, red water so still it might be Jell-O, into which The Mother had accidentally fallen and cooled, just her oval face and arms and knees sticking out. She would have been happy to be so still.

A shard of The Father's broken razor, the razor that Easter smashed, fallen out of The Mother's full-of-death hand, splattering the blue tile in red dots.

The Terrible Thing. The Terrible Thing. The way that she'd wished for something like The Terrible Thing over and over again. Thought that it would fix her, transform her into someone better.

The Father probably hadn't noticed yet. But he may have. It's simply so unremarkable, so much more a nuisance than anything else, he's waiting for a more opportune time to deal with it. Like a burnt-out light bulb in a rarely used closet. He'll get around to it eventually. And Easter wished that he were the dead one, not The Mother.

"Are you sad?" asked Julia.

And I nodded. And I nodded and I nodded.

And Julia asked, "Do you want me to roll the rock off?"

And I nodded again. Even though it was supposed to be Lev who saved me. Supposed to be him so that we could walk away happily ever after and I wouldn't be lonely anymore. And he would invite me underground to have dinner with his family in their very dark dining room. But it was Julia who was here and Julia who I really loved. So she rolled the rock off. And my legs were perfectly fine, full of blood and life and all the electricity that a young girl's legs should be full of. I got up, with Julia's help, and made my way toward the path.

"Where are you going?" she asked.
"The House."
"You aren't going back to Mrs. Bellows'?"
"No."
"How come?"

"Because someone needs to do something about The Mother."

"Who are you supposed to call?"

"Phyllis, maybe? She'll know what to do."

Julia nodded.

"Are you okay?" she asked.

I shrugged. "I don't know yet."

And Julia nodded.

I'd go back to The Tooth House and I'd call Phyllis and then probably the hospital.

And then I'd stay in The Tooth House with The Father and I'd live upstairs the way that she had. And he'd live downstairs like always.

And there was no room for Julia anymore because I was all full of bugs. And they were moving around in there, making me less lonely. Little implants whose little legs would polish me into someone who felt better and acted better. More normal. Powered by the bell, which rang somewhere always whether I heard it or not. Ceaseless so a person hardly notices. Like the twittering leaves all day long.

It had transformed from a hot June day to a cool June night. My feet crunched into the forest floor. Julia followed close behind, squirrels hopping around her feet, following too in their way, but I knew she wouldn't leave The Woods. She belonged in here now, my sliver in the universe, and this is where I'd keep her from now on.

Acknowledgments

Very special thanks to Lisa Samuels, Ali McDonald, and Brian Farrey-Latz for making this book happen, and to all my early readers: Paul Clairmont, Delia Byrnes, Heidi Tannenbaum, Sam Swenson, Alex Hartley, Madison Hogarth, and my parents Debbie and Tom Hogarth. THANK YOU!

Photo by Paul Clairmont

About the Author

Ainslie Hogarth was born and raised in Windsor, Ontario, but currently resides in Toronto. She has an undergraduate degree in English Literature and Philosophy and a Masters in Creative Writing. She watches a lot of movies and has a lot more books in her head. *The Lonely* is her debut novel. Visit her online at ainsliehogarth.com.